THE SECRET 6:
THE MONSTER MURDERS

THE SECRET 6

THE MONSTER MURDERS

By Robert J. Hogan

STEEGER BOOKS • 2020

PUBLISHING HISTORY

"The Monster Murders" originally appeared in the December, 1934 (Vol. 1, No. 3) issue of *The Secret 6* magazine. Copyright 2020 by Argosy Communications, Inc. All rights reserved.

CHAPTER 1
THE GIANT DOGS

IT WAS evening. Members of the Secret 6 band were seated about the cabin. All were present except The Key. Luga, the giant Zulu chief, was preparing their evening meal when King tossed a cigarette into the fireplace and shook his head.

"I confess," he said, "I'm worried. The Key has had entirely too much to say about those old records that were stolen from the district attorney's office."

"Surely," said the Bishop, "you don't think that he had anything to do with their disappearance?"

King shook his head. "I never make accusations, Bishop, unless I am certain. The thing that sticks in my mind is that he's been too interested. And he's had that wise grin covering his face for several days."

"I'm sure," the Bishop said stoutly, "when the Key has investigated the matter thoroughly to his own satisfaction he'll let us in on whatever secrets he may have."

The Doctor spoke up in his deep voice. "I can't see any reason why The Key should be so excited, either. The records that disappeared are all twenty to thirty years old."

King looked thoughtfully into the fire for a time. After a minute he nodded.

"I think," he said with finality, "as soon as supper is over I'll drive down to New York."

"Certainly," the Bishop exclaimed, "you wouldn't expect to locate The Key immediately?"

"Hardly," agreed King. "But the Key's been gone since last night. I propose to contact every one of the five who keep us posted with their short wave sending sets. I'll gamble The Key has seen some of them today."

Luga called them to dinner and they sat down. King ate silently. When he was through he pushed back his plate and rose. Luga stood attentively by his side.

"I go with you, Master?"

It was an earnest question. King shrugged.

"Just as you please, big boy," he said. "I don't know if there will be anything for you to do. You can drive the car if you want."

"Suppose," suggested the Doctor, "we all go. Perhaps some of us might take in a show while you do your private investigating. I certainly don't propose to waste my time on such a foolish mission."

"You may be perfectly right," said King. "Perhaps it's just curiosity that's driving me along to this." He turned toward the door. "Well, I'm ready if the rest of you are. Let's go."

They walked in single file through the woods to the spot

The monster dog leaped at Luga.

where the two cars were hidden. It was a cleared opening surrounded by trees and bushes at the end of a bedrock drive on which tire marks did not show.

The big roadster was gone. The Key had taken it the night before when he drove into town. They climbed into the little sedan and Luga took the wheel. King sat beside him.

"Where we go first, Master?" Luga asked some fifty minutes later as they crossed the bridge into Manhattan and turned downtown.

"I think the first stop will be Flo's apartment," King answered. "She's up in the seventies."

"Yes, Master."

The car turned east on 77th; except for the street lights, it was pitch dark. Not a light shown in any of the buildings. King frowned.

"Wait a minute," he said, just as Luga was pulling up in front of Flo's apartment house. "That's funny. This whole street seems deserted. Do you see anyone?"

There was a pause and before Luga answered, "No, Master, Luga not—Wait. Yes, Luga see someone. Over there in the shadow on the sidewalk. See?"

King gasped. "That's not a human being," he exclaimed. "Can you see it plainly? Swing over that way, Luga."

The car swerved toward the spot where the figure was moving.

"By George!" exploded the Doctor. "It looks like a horse."

"It's a four-legged beast of some kind," King decided. "I wish he'd get in the light of that street lamp so we could see him. Why under the sun is a horse trotting on the sidewalk?"

4

"Animal stop now, Master," Luga said.

That was true.

The great four-footed animal had stopped just at a point where the shadow and street light blinded them so they couldn't see it.

"Drive on closer," King ordered.

Then the animal did an astonishing thing. It lifted its head toward the street light above. The giant mouth opened and a strange sound came out, echoing against the walls of the cavernous street.

It was a sound like the howl of a dog, but far deeper. It was as though the voice of a dog had been deepened and amplified five times. There were three long howls and then a series of deep, bellowing barks. King gasped.

"The thing's a monster!" he exclaimed. "Look, he acts as if he's turning to run. Stop the car, Luga!"

King leaped out, started on a dead run for the animal. Luga was on his heels. The other three members of the Secret 6 band were close behind. They saw the dog clearly now that they had passed the street light.

He stood as high as a fair-sized saddle horse. The great eyes glared at them.

A giant tongue came out as he licked his chops. Then he crouched with an angry, deep-throated growl. Dimly they could see the stiff hair on his back bristle.

"Look out!" yelled King. "He's coming for us!"

At the same time he whipped out his automatic. Scarcely

thirty feet separated them from the giant dog. Two or three more bounds and he would be upon them.

Blam! Blam! Blam!

King's automatic spit flame and the bellow of the explosions echoed hollowly through the canyon street. He couldn't tell in the darkness whether he had hit the dog or not. At least it was coming on, growling more ferociously than ever. Its great fanged mouth was gaping wide. One more leap and it would be there! That mouth was large enough to take a man's head inside and crush it with little effort.

King was crouching, taking aim more carefully this time.

Blam! Blam!

THE AUTOMATIC bellowed out again. The dog was on his last spring now. Savage fangs snapped. King leaped side-wise to escape the terrific onrush.

Luga tried to follow him, but the move brought him right into the path of the leaping dog. King saw him go down with the dog on top. Then the two were bounding so closely that he couldn't tell which was which. He didn't dare fire for fear of hitting Luga.

He only saw a desperate struggle there in the darkness; a struggle that lasted but a moment. Then the mass that was composed of black humanity and giant dog rolled over.

He saw the great black man striking. Saw a blade gleaming in his hand. The hind legs of the huge dog kicked twice. Then the body quivered and lay still. King was at the side of his faithful black.

"Are you hurt, Luga?"

"No, Master," panted the Zulu chief. "Luga get him. Your shots help."

They were staring down at the dog in the light of flashlights.

"It looks," said the Doctor, "like a giant mongrel."

Then suddenly all five of them tensed as they stood about the body of the animal. Through the silence they heard the padding of heavy feet. Dark shadows were coming from either end of the street. Shadows that were as large as the dim shape that this huge animal had made when they first saw him. Two were approaching from one end of the street. One was coming from the other.

"They're answering the howls of this beast we just killed!" King decided. "There must be a whole pack of them! Quick! Get out your guns, all of you that are armed."

Guns came out. Men of the Secret 6 stooped, took aim, fired. One of the dogs fell in a heap. The other two came on. Shots rang out again. Another dog dropped. The third leaped at them. Its fangs were wide and its snarl was louder than that of a lion.

Blam! Blam! Blam!

Guns barked again and then Luga leaped straight for the dog. That same knife, dripping with blood, gleamed in his hand. It flashed back and forth in rapid succession.

The dog was snarling furiously. Its teeth clicked and clicked again as it snapped at the black man who was finishing him. They rolled over and over. Rolled into the street. Then Luga got to his feet.

At the same time a voice called out, "Hey, what's going on? Where do you think you are? In Africa?"

7

A figure strode across the street. A small, slim figure and the face had a nose that was bent. It was the Key.

"Where have you been?" King demanded.

The Key grinned and shrugged.

"Just browsing around on a little investigation of my own," he answered. "I just been up to see Flo to give her orders for the night. What's all this shooting about?"

"Take a look," said King. "Did you ever see dogs as big as that?"

The Key stared. "Well, I'll be da-darned!" he exclaimed and grinned at the Bishop. "I didn't know they made purps that big."

"They don't," said the Doctor.

"Huh? Listen, I haven't been drinking and I'm looking at those big flea-hounds right now."

Then for the first time since their arrival a car turned into the street from the next block. The driver was making a familiar sound as he drove slowly along. He was whistling the characteristic whistle that a man makes when he calls his dog.

"Wait," King ordered. "Quick, Doctor. What do you make of these dead dogs? Could they be an almost extinct type, perhaps imported from a foreign country?"

The Doctor shook his head.

"No, they're a bunch of mongrels. No special breed."

King nodded, and then he deliberately stepped out before the car, which had almost reached them. The auto slowed abruptly. King peered at the man behind the wheel.

"Who are you?" he demanded, "and what are you looking for?"

The driver—a small, alert-eyed man—looked back at him sharply.

"I'm Dr. Rhinehart. I live a block or so away. Good heavens!" he went on, as he sighted the carcasses of the giant dogs lying on the sidewalk, "What are those things? They look like dead horses."

"They're not," King said. "They're dogs!"

Dr. Rhinehart hesitated, then he repeated, "Dogs—why—"

King interrupted him. "Dr. Rhinehart, you just drove down this street whistling for a dog. What do you know about these giant canines?"

"What do I know about them?" Dr. Rhinehart asked. "Why should I know anything about them? I came down here whistling for my dog, that's true. But he's only a little Boston Bull. He got away from his leash earlier tonight and disappeared. I've been hunting all over the section for him."

He was opening the door of his car, getting out.

"By George! This is interesting, isn't it? Huge dogs like that." He walked over and inspected them. "And they don't seem to be of any particular breed either, do they? What do you make of it, gentlemen?"

"That's what we're asking you?" said King.

"But why me?" asked Rhinehart in astonishment. Then he laughed. "Surely you don't think I have anything to do with these giant creatures! After all, I'm simply a doctor of medicine, not a collector of freak animals."

King nodded reluctantly.

"I guess you're right, doctor. It does seem rather ridiculous to tie you up with a bunch of huge dogs."

"It's rather a good joke," chuckled Dr. Rhinehart. "Imagine a person starting out in a coupé to round up four dogs the size of these. Their owner should be out looking for them with a horse truck!"

The sound of a police siren sounded down the street. Any number of persons in that block had probably reported the shooting. The Key was tugging at King's arm.

"Come on," he hissed in a low voice. "You guys better haul out of here if you know what's good for you. I've got the roadster in front of Flo's apartment. I'll drive it back to the jungle. Let's scram before it's too late. The Dummy will give us the dope."

THE FIVE climbed into the sedan while The Key ran across the street to the roadster. Engines were started. They moved away hurriedly. King watched the doctor as he climbed into his car and moved on. He shook his head.

"I almost wish we'd had more time to question that bird," he said.

"I fear you grow too suspicious of everyone," ventured the Bishop. "I for one have lived in the city a great deal of my life, and I can assure you that there are many people out at this time of night calling their pet animals that have strayed away."

"One thing stumps me," King said as he turned the corner and the police sirens died. "Why was it that the police took so long in getting here? I expected them long before now."

He got his answer when he drove two blocks north and

turned into another street. Shots echoed down the block. Three police cars were there.

And they heard, mingled with the sound of the shots, the howls and barks of dogs. They could see their giant shadowy forms as they ran headlong—some of them to escape their attackers, others to leap upon them.

"Stop! Stop the car!" King yelled. He was out in a flash and the members of the Secret 6 battled the dogs together.

When all the giant dogs that they could see were dead, King and his men climbed back into the car. Street after street was the scene of battle. Here and there a dog leaped out of the darkness.

There were no pedestrians in sight, except those who had gone to their apartments to procure weapons and had returned to fight the giant dog menace.

For an hour or more they cruised the uptown streets looking for more of the monsters. But they found none. At length, in the early hours of the morning, they turned out to Long Island. The Key was not yet at their retreat when they reached it.

They turned in for a short sleep and when they awoke The Key greeted them. He grinned as he tossed a late edition of the morning paper down on the table.

"You can take my tip, gang," he said, "there's a case to sink your teeth in."

King picked up one of the papers. Great scareheads across the front glared at him.

GIANT DOGS AT LARGE

Dogs as Large as Horses Kill Several in Uptown Manhattan—
Humanity Flees Before Horde of Monster Canines

"New York: Uptown Manhattan was terrorized early this morning when huge beasts were seen roaming the streets. At first it was thought horses had escaped from a milk stable nearby, but on closer investigation it was found that the animals were dogs. At an early hour it was reported that two residents of that vicinity had been attacked and horribly mutilated as they were on their way home from the 79th Street subway station."

"Yes," King admitted. "That's a case all right. But apparently we know more about it than this reporter did."

"Naw," said The Key, "that isn't what I'm talking about. It's the other story."

CHAPTER 2
SUICIDE?

AS THE Key spoke, he pointed to another headline on the front page.

BANKER POSSIBLE SUICIDE

Strange Circumstances Take Place Before Body Is Found

"New York: Horace Mann, president of the International Bank, was thought to have committed suicide early this morning. Blackmail was hinted.

"Patrolman Michael Kelly on his regular beat about the palatial home of the bank president, reported that shortly before midnight a man, well over six feet in height, left the residence. A huge dog came out of the shadows and followed him.

"The patrolman says at first he thought the dog was chasing the man, and remembering the giant dog menace, he shot the animal. As the dog fell, the large man broke into a run. The patrolman ordered him to stop, but the man escaped.

"It is believed now that this man had a direct connection with the giant dogs, and that the dog was following him as a pet would follow its master."

"I'm afraid," ventured the Bishop, "the whole thing is a bit vague in my mind."

The Key snorted. "To me it's plain that the whole thing ties up with those records that disappeared from the D.A.'s office. I think this is just the beginning of a swell blackmail racket."

"I suppose you've already made investigation, Key," the Bishop said, "among your friends in the city?"

"You're da—darned right," the Key nodded. "I told the Dummy to keep us posted on anything that turned up at police headquarters. And I got hold of Flo the Fleecer last night and told her to find out all she could about certain citizens of the big dump who are in the blackmail racket. We ought to be getting some info soon."

King shook his head. "Just how do you figure all this ties together? The dogs and the suicide of Horace Mann and the disappearance of records from the District Attorney's office?"

"Well, of course, I'm just guessing," the Key admitted, "but I look at it this way. The cops think that Horace Mann committed suicide because of a blackmail threat made by the big guy who was seen coming out of his house near midnight. Kelly says the huge dog followed the guy away like a pet.

"Well, there ain't any sweeter proposition for blackmail than those stolen records from the D.A.'s office. And the fact that one of the purps seemed to be a pet of the guy who was blackmailing Mann makes me think the whole layout is tied up together somehow."

King turned his head so that his keen eyes fell on the little man's face.

"Key," he said, "why did you suspect blackmail when those records first disappeared?"

"Huh," growled the Key, "you wouldn't have to ask that if you knew some of these lugs like I do. Since Prohibition went out, the dough don't flow like it used to. There is certain citizens who used to make plenty out of the beer and liquor business. Now there ain't nothing much left for them to do but peddle papers or sell lead pencils."

"Yes, I know," the Doctor flared, "but what has that got to do with moth-eaten records stolen from the District Attorney's office?"

The Key shrugged.

"It's just a hunch. I know what I'd do with a lot of old records."

The Bishop's eyes twinkled. "Pardon me. I believe you mean you know what you might have done in years past before you saw the light of going straight."

The Key nodded.

"Sure, sure," he agreed, "that's what I mean Bishop. Hel—I mean goodness, I wouldn't think of it now. But just for fun,

Bishop, let's say I was back pulling some of the old deals. Now suppose I was walking along the street and I see some old books fall out of a truck. You know, just happen to find them. Course I wouldn't steal them or nothing."

Everyone about the table smiled.

"You know there's an awful lot of guys," the Key went on, "that have been hooked up with the D.A.'s office in the past when they were young and foolish. Maybe they was perfectly innocent. Take one guy I know of. He was a bookkeeper in a small bank. The president pulled some phony stuff and framed this guy. And believe me that clerk had one swell job making the D.A. believe he was innocent. But somebody in the D.A.'s office was a relative of the bank president's wife, and when they found out that the president was in on the deal the whole thing was kind of squashed on condition that the president would resign. Which he did.

"Well, this bookkeeper guy kept his job but he always had that shadow hanging over him because the case had never been tried. His vindication was kept out of the papers on account of the bank president's wife. He worked his way up to cashier, and finally became the president of one of the big banks in New York."

The Key sat back and lighted a cigarette.

"You mean to tell me," he grinned, "that I couldn't collect plenty of dough if I threatened to publish the old scandal straight from the D.A.'s records?"

Shakespeare cleared his throat.

"Young man," he said, "I believe you are correct. If a story like that got out, especially at this time, it would shatter the faith of depositors—ruin the bank."

"SURE," THE Key nodded, eagerly. "This bank president makes a salary of about one hundred grand a year. He'd be da— darn glad to pay me $10,000 a year to keep my mouth shut. Why, if I had those records I could track down every guy that had been even questioned by the D.A. twenty or thirty years ago. And I'll bet I could dig out doctors and lawyers, and bank presidents, and manufacturers, and heads of corporations and a whole flock of big shots that had at some time or other been mixed up in some scandal—lots of them innocently. But when you get to be a big shot you can't afford to have anything come out that's going to be a blot on your name.

"And I'd pick guys that were making so much dough now that a few grand a year paid to me to keep my mouth shut wouldn't mean a thing in their life."

King nodded slowly.

"I can see some logic in that," he said.

While he spoke, the Doctor had walked over to the short wave receiver and turned it on. There was a low whistling sound, which cleared presently into a mumbled voice. Every man in the room tensed.

The mumbling sound resolved itself into a monotone. It was weird in its monotony. There was no inflection of words or phrases. It was as though a deaf man had learned to talk—which was exactly the case with the Dummy.

"Hello Secret 6. Hello Secret 6, Hello Secret 6." The voice groaned. "This is the Dummy. The Dummy. Can you hear me?

16

Got dope from police headquarters. Listen. Police think suicide of Horace Mann caused by blackmail and hook up with stolen D.A. records. Thirty years ago Mann was questioned on thefts in bank where he worked. President of bank shot himself and case was dropped. If case was brought up now might ruin Mann's position. Stolen records are thirty years old. Got it? Police going to keep this story out of the papers. Looking for tall man that Patrolman Kelly saw leaving Horace Mann's house. Lookin' for more giant dogs as possible key to the big man."

The radio hummed for a few seconds longer. Then the hum stopped. The Key grinned and shrugged.

"Well, what kind of a guesser am I now?" he demanded. "Did I guess right or did I guess right? But of course some of you mugs wouldn't believe me until you got it from the police. Wouldn't that be a swell headline in the paper. SECRET 6 WORK ON INFORMATION GAINED FROM POLICE."

"That wouldn't be so funny," King corrected. "Personally I wish we could work closer with the police, but as long as they think we are a bunch of cutthroats there isn't much of a chance."

The Bishop looked serious for a moment.

"I was wondering, gentlemen," he said, "if our past deeds have not proved us worthy of the confidence of the police. It would facilitate matters much more, as King suggests, if we could work with them rather than in spite of them. I've been thinking rather seriously of meeting the police commissioner and having a talk with him."

"Not a chance," the Key laughed, "boy, I wish I had the confidence in human nature that you've got, Bishop. They'll grab you and throw you in the jug before you can say Hokus Pokus. Don't forget that you were the guy who got me and King out of the death house a while ago. The cops won't ever get over that."

King smiled.

"I think the Key is right," he said. "It's a nice idea and all that, but I'm afraid we'd better forget it."

Suddenly the radio began hissing again, took life. A mellow feminine voice began drifting into the room.

"Hello Secret 6. Flo talking. How are you? I saw the Key last night and he asked me to browse around a bit, so I did. Did any of you ever hear of Mark Fiddler? He's known to the underworld as a small time blackmailer. For a year or so, around the end of the war, he got pretty big in that game. Then he left it for the liquor racket, but I guess when Prohibition went out again he didn't have much dough. He had quite a gang and tried two or three blackmail stunts. None of them worked out. But here's what happened last night.

"I went up to visit a friend who lives in the apartment next to him. I looked at the clock. It was about eleven o'clock. We heard an awful commotion. It sounded like a fist fight. We finally went to the door and peeked out just in time to see Fiddler's door open and a huge man stalk out. He was very tall and stooped as he walked. He carried a heavy bundle under his arm. The elevator is self-operated so it is quite possible that we were the only ones who saw him leave the apartment house.

"We went to Fiddler's apartment fearing that he might be dead. He was lying on the floor of the living room. His face was beaten almost to a pulp but he wasn't dead. He was lying there groaning, so we hurried away before he could open his eyes and see us. We thought of calling the hospital and then we were afraid to because we didn't want to get mixed up in some private affair of Fiddler's. So we just left him there. Maybe this won't interest you but I promised to report anything that I learned and there it is. I'll try to get on the track of some other blackmailers as soon as I can spot them. This is Flo signing off."

AS THE radio went dead the members of the Secret 6 stared at each other, puzzled.

"By George," King explained, "I wonder if this big fellow could have any connection with the man who was seen leaving Horace Mann's home."

The Key grinned.

"Well, if he hasn't," he chuckled, "I'll kiss your foot at Times Square three o'clock in the afternoon. It's a cinch. This big mug goes to Mark Fiddler and beats him to a fare-you-well. Fiddler is probably the guy who engineered the stealing of those old records. The big mug looks through the records and sees that Horace Mann thirty years ago was hooked up with a bank scandal. So he goes to Horace Mann and tells him that if he doesn't give him some dough he'll publish the whole story. Then he walks out and leaves him to think it over. And Mann being a very wise guy knows that if he starts paying this big mug, he won't have any peace the rest of his life.

"So he thinks it over for about an hour. Then he puts a gun to his head and lets go. And you can take it from me that's just a start of what's going to happen all over New York."

King shook his head.

"It doesn't tie together, Key," he said.

"Huh!" growled the Key in astonishment.

"No," King repeated, "it doesn't tie together. Look here. It would take this big man at least fifteen or twenty minutes to get from the apartment house where Mark Fiddler lives up to the residence of Horace Mann. And he'd have to travel in a taxi to do it that fast.

"If he left Mann's house around midnight, he must have arrived at least fifteen or twenty minutes before. Suppose you were putting over a black mail deal, what would you do? You'd go up to the man's home, be ushered in. It would take a minute or two to get an audience with him. Then you'd start explaining your proposition. He'd argue and you'd try to convince him. You'd finally leave him with the pleasant idea that he'd either pay you the money or else he'd be ruined within the next twenty-four hours. All of which would take at least fifteen or twenty minutes."

The Key nodded, "Yeah, I guess that's right."

"All of which," King said, "proves to me that this bird who beat up Mark Fiddler wasn't the same one who was seen by Patrolman Kelly leaving the home of Horace Mann."

Then King sat back. Puffed at his cigarette and smiled.

"Unless," he went on—

CHAPTER 3
THE SEVEN-FOOT MAN

"UNLESS WHAT," demanded the Key. "Well, I have been thinking of another angle," King said. "Let's assume that he did do both jobs. Flo said it was about 11 o'clock when the fight started in Mark Fiddler's apartment. It probably lasted for ten minutes, perhaps fifteen. For the sake of argument let's say ten. It would take the victor twenty minutes to reach Mann's house from there by taxi. That would be half past eleven."

Heads nodded in agreement as the Secret 6 followed his argument.

"We've assumed that the big fellow stayed with Mann at least fifteen or twenty minutes."

Heads nodded again.

"Why that," exclaimed the Bishop, "would leave this giant-sort of a chap only fifteen minutes at the most to look through the records and find that Horace Mann had been mixed up in a scandal thirty years before."

King smiled.

"That's exactly what I'm driving at," he announced. "It is incredible. Several volumes of records were stolen—enough to constitute the heavy bundle that Flo saw this big fellow taking from Mark Fiddler's apartment. But how anyone could wade through a group of volumes like that in ten or fifteen minutes, find Horace Mann's name as a possible subject for blackmail, look up his address and run up to see him is beyond me. It would

21

take hours—days—to go through those records and pick out the most likely victims."

"It would," growled the Doctor. "There's no connection between the two. We're just getting worked up for nothing."

"Oh," King said, "I didn't say that. Figure it out from this angle—that the big man is the one who stole the volumes in the first place. Then the chances are that he has made a study of them long before and had already spotted his victims."

"But where," the Key demanded, "would Mark Fiddler fit into the picture?"

King shrugged.

"I haven't the slightest idea. If you'll let your imagination run, Fiddler might fit in several capacities. For instance, he might have gotten wind of the thing, found the thief and stolen the records from him. When the big fellow learned his identity, he beat him up, took back the records and started his blackmail program right away."

"That," said the Bishop, "sounds very plausible."

"Yes," agreed Shakespeare, "the blackmailer must have spent considerable time studying the evidence."

The Key grinned at the Doctor.

"Maybe I ain't so dumb after all."

The Doctor simply growled.

"You remember, Key, who was suspected of stealing those records?" King asked.

The Key thought for a moment then he got up and rummaged in a pile of newspapers in one corner of the cabin. He found one, a paper more than two weeks old, and handed it to King, who read aloud from the headlines.

"Former clerk of the District Attorney's office suspected!

"Henry Gilson, for years a trusted clerk of the District Attorney's office has not been seen or heard of since the old records disappeared. At present Gilson is being hunted by the police. It is suspected by the authorities that his arrest will throw light upon the disappearance."

King nodded.

"I think," he said, "there's where we've got to start. It's queer the Dummy didn't say something about this. Surely the police would figure that Gilson is behind this thing that happened last night."

"But," the Bishop pointed out, "the police might not suspect as much as we do if they don't know the large man beat up Mark Fiddler last night. Do you think they do?"

"I doubt it very much," King said. "Flo and her friend say they didn't call authorities or the hospital. Apparently no one else did or she would have mentioned it. Birds like Mark Fiddler don't very often ask the police to help them. But even at that I can't figure it out. If this fellow, Henry Gilson, is six feet three or four, how could he escape detection so long? A man that size stands out like a sore thumb anywhere."

"The police are awful dumb sometimes," the Doctor ventured.

"Perhaps in a few cases, yes," King said as he shook his head. "But not ordinarily."

King got up and stretched. He reached for his coat, slipped it on, straightened his tie.

"I think," he said, "this job will stand a little investigation."

Luga was beside him instantly.

"Luga go with you," he pleaded.

King smiled as he shook his head.

"I'm afraid not, big boy," he said. "At night when it's dark and I'm always delighted, but you'd be just like this other big man we're talking about. You'd stand out too much in a crowd. I think I'll take you along, Key. And, Shakespeare, how about a little makeup for each of us, so we won't stand out too much in the crowd ourselves?"

"Very well," agreed Shakespeare, "it shall be a pleasure."

THEY RECLINED in easy chairs while Shakespeare worked on their faces for a few minutes with deft touches of makeup brush and stick. He changed their appearances so that they would not be easily recognized. When he was through King and the Key got up, waved a farewell to the other members of their loyal band and walked out into the crisp morning air.

The Key growled disgustedly as they strode through the woods.

"Huh, the Doctor think's I'm leading you on a wild goose chase."

"Well, it didn't look very hot at first," King said. "But it seems now as though we're getting somewhere. This big man proposition has certainly got me buffaloed. Here's a man that would be head and shoulders above an ordinary crowd and still he steals the records from the D.A.'s office and then starts putting the blackmail finger on one of the most prominent bankers in the country."

"What are you going to do?" the Key asked.

"I haven't quite made up my mind," King said. "I'll think it over as we drive down to the city. If I dared chance it I'd go down to the D.A.'s office and get the whole story."

They reached their two cars. King climbed into the roadster and the Key settled in the seat beside him. The motor purred. The car backed out and started down the secret bed rock drive. Just before they hit the main road, the Key descended, walked ahead to the highway and glanced up and down. A truck rumbled past, then an old touring car passed, and then another. After that the Key motioned King that the road was clear. He hopped aboard as the roadster swung on to the main thoroughfare and turned east.

King pushed the accelerator down till the car was hitting 60 miles an hour and held it there. His mind was working like mad trying to figure out the details of the problem. The whole thing was beginning to have a weird aspect. Somehow it looked like an open and shut proposition.

Henry Gilson was beyond doubt the man they were after. He was the blackmailer who had beat up Mark Fiddler and had caused Horace Mann to commit suicide. It must be so—and yet King had a feeling that that wasn't the case.

The traffic grew heavier as he neared the metropolitan center. He drove through Brooklyn, crossed the bridge over into Manhattan and turned downtown. He was trying to figure out his plans in the proper sequence. He wanted to stop and have a talk with Flo the Fleecer. He planned to go to the apartment of Mark Fiddler and learn from that king blackmailer what he knew about the situation. He wanted to get a description of Henry Gilson from the District Attorney's office.

Flo lived well uptown. Mark Fiddler's apartment was below on 56th Street, the District Attorney's office further down. He decided to stop and see Flo first. The car pulled up in front of her apartment house and King got out. The Key shot him a parting grin.

"Watch out boy," he warned, "that beautiful dame will get you one of these days. She gets them all."

King laughed.

"She's a good scout," he said, "but I think Flo and I understand each other."

He went inside, stepped into the elevator and was shot up to Flo's floor. He waited several minutes after he knocked on her door before she opened it a crack to peer out. Instantly she flung it wide.

"Why didn't you tell me you were coming," she smiled. "I would have put on my best party dress."

King laughed. "I was afraid you would be asleep and I didn't want to disturb your beauty slumbers any more than necessary."

Flo looked entrancing and surprisingly fresh in an orchid negligee, as though she had gotten a good night's rest, which she hadn't. Her hair was all out of order but it made her seem even more lovely.

"You didn't get much sleep last night," King said.

"How could I?" she countered. "I was watching the Fiddler's

apartment all night. But I managed to get a wink or two this morning after I sent you the message. Did the information help?"

"I think so," King told her. "Did you by any chance connect what you saw to the Mann suicide that occurred shortly afterward?"

She shook her head.

"I hadn't thought of it that way."

He lighted a cigarette and looked at it thoughtfully for a moment.

"Patrolman Kelly," he said, "was reported to have seen a man over six feet tall coming out of Horace Mann's. I want to check up with Kelly himself."

A frightened look came into the girl's eyes.

"You don't mean you're going direct to the police, King? Why they'll nab you in a minute."

King laughed.

"I don't expect to wear a name printed on me like a good Rotarian at a luncheon," he chuckled. "Would you know this big man if you saw him again?"

"I'm sure of it," declared Flo. "He's the biggest man I've ever seen in my life."

"Then he must be more than six feet three or four," King said. "Some doormen for New York hotels and theaters are taller than that."

Flo stopped to think for a moment.

"Perhaps," she admitted, "I under-measured him. I remember now that he stooped as he came out of the door. He had to in order to get out."

King frowned.

"Are those doors lower than other doors?"

"I don't think so," Flo said. "They looked ordinary size to me."

"Then this man must have been almost seven feet."

"Perhaps he was," Flo agreed. "Gladys, that's my girlfriend, and I were so excited by the time the fight had stopped, that we didn't observe very accurately. Yes, I'm sure he stooped coming out of the door. Come to think about it, he stooped as he walked through the hall."

"Then he might have been seven feet tall," King said.

The girl nodded. "Yes, it's very possible."

"Phew!" King whistled. "What a man he would be to run up against in a dark alley. And you say he was rather heavily built?"

"He certainly wasn't skinny. He was the most powerful brute of a man I've ever seen."

King smiled. "You've been to circuses?" he asked.

"Yes, and I've lived around New York all of my life where there is about as much strange humanity as one sees anywhere."

King got up and smiled.

"Thanks a lot, Flo. I think now I'll run over and have a little talk with your friend's neighbor, Mark Fiddler. Maybe he can tell me something about this giant."

The girl's eyes took on a frightened look again.

"You mean you're going to walk right in face to face and ask him what it is all about?"

"Oh, not exactly that," King said. "I don't mean to go in and slap him in the face with a hearty 'Hello, Mark, how are you?' But I would like to get a slant on what he thinks about it."

"I don't think you will," the girl said. "You're taking an unnecessary chance."

"That's part of the game," King smiled. "Thanks for what you have done, Flo. I'll be seeing you."

He had gotten up and turned toward the door now. The girl walked with him.

"Please, I wish you wouldn't take these unnecessary chances, King. You're too good a guy to get bumped off."

King laughed.

"Flo," he said, "if you think I have any ambitions toward getting bumped off you're wrong. But I do want to face this Fiddler bird. Keep the home fires burning, Flo, until you hear from us."

The girl smiled a little.

"I'm afraid," she said, "Mark Fiddler will make it a lot hotter for you over in his apartment than any home fire I can keep burning. But good luck, anyway."

Then King went out and down the elevator. He met the Key and took the wheel of the car himself.

"What do you figure now?" asked the Key.

"I'm not figuring anything until I've had a talk with Mark Fiddler and then gone down to the D.A.'s office and talked with them and—"

"Holy gee," exploded the Key, "you're not—"

"Sure," said King, "why not? We've got to find out things and the only way to do that is to go to the bottom of them."

He drew up in front of the apartment house on 56th Street where Mark Fiddler lived. They sat there for a moment.

"Keep track of that watch on the dash," King said earnestly. "If I'm not down in fifteen minutes come up after me. You've got a good automatic in your pocket and you know how to use it. Only don't get heavy-fingered on the trigger unless it is absolutely necessary."

The Key opened his mouth to say something, perhaps to argue. But King was gone before he could get the words out.

CHAPTER 4
TRAPPED

KING TRIED the door of the apartment house; it was locked. He studied the rows of buttons with mail boxes below them. Found Mark Fiddler's card in one. Next to it was the name of Miss Gladys Johnson. He smiled. That must be Flo's friend. He pushed the bell below Gladys' card, listened in the speaking tube but no sound came. He pushed the bell again and again. Gladys Johnson was evidently not at home.

A slow smile spread over his face. Perhaps he might fool some other woman in the house. It was worth trying. He found another name—Miss Greta Farnham. His smile broadened as he pushed the bell. Then a feminine voice came twanging metallically through the speaking-tube into his ears.

"Hello," King spoke very softly. "It's me, Greta. Open the door will you?"

"Oh, is that you, Billy?"

"Yes."

"All right," the girl answered, "just a minute."

The latch on the door began to buzz. King pushed it open and went inside. He entered into a little lobby from which a staircase went up on either side; at the back there were two self-operated elevators. One was open. He stepped inside, pushed the button for the sixth floor where Mark Fiddler lived. The elevator crawled up. Getting out on the sixth floor he studied the numbers on the doors. Mark Fiddler's was in plain sight of the elevators. He glanced at the next door. That was probably the one from which Flo and her friend had watched the monster after he had left Fiddler's room.

King hesitated before the door of Fiddler's apartment. Then he took a long breath and knocked. He heard a mumble of voices on the other side, then the knob turned and the door flew open.

A swarthy individual with a silk shirt and neatly-fitting clothes glared at him.

"What do you want?" he demanded.

King tensed. He could look past the man who had opened it and in the living room he saw two other figures. One was a hard-looking character; the other was seated in a chair. His face was purple and blue and black in blotches—the face of a man beaten almost beyond recognition.

King jerked his head toward the figure in the chair.

"I want to see Fiddler," he said.

"Oh, you do, do you," snapped the man at the door. "Who are you?"

31

King stepped forward until he had his foot in the crack of the door, and waved a jovial greeting.

"Hi, Fiddler," he said, "I've got something to tell you."

He saw that the man at the door had his right hand in his coat pocket and there seemed to be a bulge larger than his hand would make.

"What do you want," Fiddler demanded in a thick voice.

"Pull this mug out of my way," King called, "and I'll tell you. Do you expect me to stand out in the hall and shout it to all of your neighbors?"

"Let him come in," Fiddler said.

The man at the door stepped aside but his eyes never left King's face. The second man had stepped to the other side and his hand was in his pocket too. King was covered from both angles.

But he swaggered in with a jaunty cocksure air. Much more than he felt inside. He walked up to Fiddler and grinned in his face.

"Boy," he said, "that big guy must have beaten you up something awful last night."

Both of Fiddler's eyes were almost swollen shut but there was an effort to narrow them still more as he stared at King menacingly.

"What do you mean? Who told you anything about a big guy beating me up last night?" he demanded.

King shrugged.

"Well don't worry. I'm not going to let the story out to the rest of the guys. Funny how news travels, ain't it?"

He came a little closer, lowered his voice to confidential tones.

"And listen, Fiddler," he went on, "if you'll give me the straight dope on this, I know where I can lay my hands on those records that the big mug stole after he beat you up."

Fiddler's eyes brightened suddenly. "Yeah?" Then suddenly his face clouded.

"Just what the devil are you talking about? What records was stolen from where?"

King grinned.

"Why you know, Fiddler. The records that was stolen out of the D.A.'s office. The old records that you were going to use for a blackmail racket. Don't try to kid me. I know the big guy took them last night and I know where they are now."

FIDDLER MOVED as though he were going to leap out of the chair. Then he growled and sank back again.

"Listen, you mug," he rasped, "if you think you can come in here and kid me just because I fell downstairs and, smashed my face you're crazy, see?" Then after a pause of perhaps two seconds. "Where are these records you're talking about?"

The two guards had moved closer with ominous stealth. They stood now with their right hands in their pockets ready to move into action on a slight notice from their boss.

King only laughed.

"That's the boy. Now you're showing some sense. You want to get those records back, don't you? Well I'm the lad that can get them for you, see? But first I want the story about this big mug so I can lay him out on a pile to rot."

33

"If you know where the records are," Fiddler growled, "you know where the big guy is. Who are you anyway?"

"What do you care?" King frowned back. "Now listen and I'll tell you something. The big mug killed my pal last night after he left here. Broke his back. And I'm going to get him if it's the last thing I do. Here's the dope. This pal of mine gets wise to the fact that the big mug is going to grab the stolen records. So he follows him, gets the records and turns and beats it. But after he hid 'em the big guy found him and broke his back like I tell you."

"I got there just as the big guy was going and found my pal dead. I know where the records are but I don't know where this big mug hangs out or who he is, see? Now if you'll tell me who he is I'll get your records for you."

King stood there waiting. He felt the black eyes of Mark Fiddler burning into his very brain. Studying him. Trying to figure out whether he was telling the truth or not. When he opened his mouth his face held a sneering expression.

"So you know where the papers are," he said. "Alright. You get the records and I'll tell you where this big guy hangs out."

King laughed.

"You must think I was born yesterday," he scoffed. "Maybe you think I'm going to let you double-cross me like you did the big guy. Don't kid yourself. I'm going to get you the records after I get the big guy, see?"

He saw Fiddler jerk his head, saw his beady eyes flashed to both of his men.

"Burn him," he growled.

The automatics were jerked out of the pockets of two on either side of him. King was covered without a chance of escape.

"Lock the door," Fiddler commanded.

One of the men walked over, turned the key in the lock and took it out. He came back, stuck his automatic in King's ribs.

King shrugged.

"Alright. You mugs kill me and you'll have a barrel of trouble on your neck. If I'm not back in half an hour my whole mob will be after me. Let those guns fly. I dare you. I've told my boys to squeal to the cops if I don't come back."

He grinned harder now at Fiddler.

"The cops will either send you to the hot seat for murdering me or they'll send you up the river for stealing the D.A. records. What do you think of that?"

Fiddler shifted uneasily in his chair. He glanced at an expensive wrist watch on his arm.

"Where's those papers?" he demanded.

King held the grin, stared back at him eye for eye.

"Who's the big guy and where's he hang out?" he countered.

For a moment Fiddler hesitated with indecision, and then jerked his head toward his two henchmen.

"You two get it out of him.

The thug on King's right stepped up, stuck the automatic in his stomach.

"Come on mug," he growled, "talk."

"Go ahead and shoot," King retorted.

The other—a stout burly fellow with heavy shoulders and arms had moved around behind him. Suddenly he made a quick move and the next second King found his arms pinned. The first man, still holding his automatic, reached down and grasped King's legs. Together they picked him up and carried him to the davenport at the end of the room.

There was no use of King struggling while those automatics were pointed at him. He knew very well that before he could fight his way clear those guns would send cold lead into his insides.

WHILE ONE held him down on the davenport, the other pulled a strap from behind the cushions, fastened him securely so that he couldn't move his arms.

The ghastliness of the situation suddenly rushed over King when they pulled off his shoes and socks. Mark Fiddler was grinning at him with one of the most hideous expressions he had ever seen on the face of a man.

"Go on," said Fiddler, "burn him until he tells where the records are."

"Listen," King snapped, "you burn me on the feet and so help me I'll never tell where those records are."

"Oh no?" growled Fiddler. "Go on. Burn him."

Very slowly the nearest thug took out a pack of cigarettes. It seemed to King that he took hours to select his cigarette.

"Here's the right one, boss," he said finally, "it's nice and full of tobacco. It will burn plenty hot."

He took a long time to tap the cigarette on the back of his hand, and then lighted a match. He let it flare until it was half burned and then lighted the cigarette and blew out the smoke.

"Think how you're going to say it," he exclaimed. "Cause you'll start talking the minute this touches your tootsie."

He puffed at the cigarette harder and harder until it glowed on the outer end, became almost white hot. Then he brought it down near King's foot.

"Come on, start talking—if you don't want to burn," he rasped.

"Hey," Fiddler said, "the lug thinks we are kidding him. Go on burn him."

King's brain was spinning rapidly. He tried desperately to think. Tried to figure out the time that had passed. Was fifteen minutes up yet? Would the Key be able to get in the apartment house? Besides, Fiddler's door was locked. How would he open it? King began stalling for time.

"Wait," he gasped, "wait until I think how to tell you where they are. Maybe I'll talk."

A rasping laugh came from Fiddler.

"Sure you'll talk," he chuckled. "I knew you would. O.K. Wait a minute, Al. But hold your cigarette so you can burn him if he changes his mind."

King jumped as something touched his foot. Then a coarse laugh from the man down there at that end of the davenport.

"If you jump like that when I touch you with my finger, what are you going to do when I burn you with a cigarette? Come on mug, talk."

Again King tried to think. It seemed that fifteen minutes ought to be up.

"Listen Fiddler," he said, stalling again. Why won't you tell me who this big guy is?"

"Because," rasped Fiddler, "that ain't any of your business."

"Well here's the reason I asked," King stalled. "I've got these papers where they're hard to get at. If you guys was to go after them you'd maybe be suspected. See what I mean? Now if you'll tell me who this big guy is I will get the records and there wouldn't be any fuss about it, see?"

"Come on. Burn him," said Fiddler. "No wait," said King, "why wouldn't you tell me about this big guy? It's a cinch you shouldn't have any love for him."

"That's my business," growled Fiddler. "Start talking."

Even now King could feel the heat from the glowing end of the cigarette against his foot. It wasn't burning enough to hurt but the pain would begin any second. If it were moved a quarter of an inch closer to his instep he knew what that would mean.

He stalled again.

"Alright," he said, "take that cigarette away and I'll tell you."

The thug removed the cigarette and puffed on it to keep it alive and hot.

"But," King went on, "don't say I didn't warn you if you get in a jam."

"We won't," growled Fiddler. "That's our business. I'm going to give you one more chance. Go on and talk or you'll get the feet burned off you."

"Alright," King said, "I live in a boarding house up at W. 86th Street. Now you go in the hall—remember, the landlady will be there and she's got a husband that's a tough egg."

"That's alright," said Fiddler. "We'll tell them we're friends of yours and that we're going to wait in your room for you."

"I don't think they'll believe you," said King. "But you can try. You go in the front hall and up the stairs. My room is on the second floor. No, it's on the third floor. They just moved me."

"Well make up your mind," snapped Fiddler. "Hey you Al. Give him a touch of heat. Maybe it will make him remember better."

King could feel the heat of the cigarette. It barely touched his instep but it felt as though a red-hot iron had been shoved all the way up his leg. He jumped and squirmed.

"Hey, wait a minute. What's the idea?" he yelled. "I'm telling you, ain't I?"

"Yeah," snarled the blackmailer, "but I think you're lying. Go on, Al, burn him good this time. Teach him a lesson."

CHAPTER 5
"STICK 'EM UP!"

"WAIT," CALLED out King, "I got it straight now. Look, get a piece of paper and I'll give you the house number and the directions. The number is 382 W. 86 and the landlady's name is Mrs. O'Toole. Tell her you want to go up to my room. When you get to the second floor, go around the hall to the back stairway. As you come up the stairs you go toward the back of the house. There is a door to the left of the stairs. That isn't the one. Mine is the next one to it. I got a room at the back that faces the yard. You can find it easy. And you can find the old records in the bottom of my clothes press under a bunch of old shoes."

Fiddler turned to his two henchmen.

"Alright, you two guys. Leave him strapped up here with me. Go down there and take a look at this place. If he is lying, we'll take the so-and-so for a ride."

The two henchmen nodded, dropped their guns into their pockets. King was watching Mark Fiddler's bruised face at the moment. Suddenly he saw

a surprised look come over it. At the same time a crisp order snapped out. King shifted his eyes and saw a familiar figure standing on the threshold.

"Alright you mugs!" It was the voice of the Key and he meant business. "Stick 'em up and reach plenty, because when I pull a trigger I never miss."

The Key stepped inside and closed the door softly behind him. The automatic gleamed in his hand. Already Fiddler's hands were going up over his head. King saw the two thugs raise theirs.

"Come on, higher," snapped the Key, "reach, I said. Remem-

"Alright, you mugs. Stick 'em up!"

ber if I unload on one of you guys I'm going to get all three of you before this gat's empty."

Fiddler and his two men did reach. Almost strained to reach the ceiling—which they couldn't touch. The faces of the two henchmen were turning ashen-white. Fiddler's face had a pallor-like look but the black and blue marks hid most of it.

The Key advanced slowly into the room. King marveled at the speed and skill with which his confederate frisked the pockets of the two thugs, all the while keeping them covered. Then, stepping behind Fiddler he took a big automatic out of a shoulder holster under his left arm-pit that was shielded by his dressing gown.

"Alright," he snarled, "line up there, one by one either side of your chief."

He glanced at the face of Fiddler and laughed. "It looks like you got what was coming for once, Fiddler," he chuckled.

"Yes," snapped Fiddler. "But this ain't over yet."

"It will be," the Key retorted, "if you don't keep your mouth shut until you're spoken to."

He crossed over to King and, with his gun still covering the three thugs, unfastened the straps that held his chief. King got up and stretched.

"Thanks for the nice rest, Mr. Fiddler," he said. "You can't say that I didn't warn you my friends knew where I was."

The henchmen that Fiddler had called Al cut in now.

"What I want to know," he rasped, "is how that squirt got through the door. You locked it, didn't you Tony?"

"Sure, I locked it," answered the other. "I got the key in my pocket. And it's one of them locks that don't open so easy." The Key's grin broadened. "Just because you mugs are dumb isn't saying that everybody is." He turned to King. "Well, what are we waiting for?" he asked.

"We're waiting," King said, "to find out about the big bird that beat up Fiddler. That is what I came here to find out and that's what I'm going to find out."

He reached into the Key's pocket and took two of the three guns that he had lifted from the thugs, dropped them into his own pockets, one in either side of his coat.

"Fiddler," he said, "before we leave here you're going to tell us who this big guy is. We're going to get it out of you if we have to stay here and keep you with your hands up over your heads until you drop."

"Alright," Fiddler growled, "keep us here and be damned. I'll never tell."

"Okay," King nodded, "suits us. Key, we might as well sit down while we are waiting. Fiddler, you stand up with the rest of them."

As King spoke he took out one of the automatics from his pocket and laid it in his lap.

"Hey," Fiddler complained, with his hands still up over his head, "I can't stand up. I was beat up too badly last night."

"That's all the more reason why you're going to stand up," King said.

He picked up the automatic and swung it so that the open end looked straight into Fiddler's face. Fiddler stood up with a groan, held his hands higher still.

"When you get ready to talk," King explained, "we'll be listening."

He glanced at the Key, saw that he had the three well covered from where he sat in an easy chair. Very calmly King took a cigarette out of a pack from his pocket. Tapped it on the back of his hand and struck a match. He puffed and calmly blew the smoke out.

"Hey, for the love of Heaven," squealed Fiddler suddenly, "you ain't going to burn me?"

King looked at him for an instant and then he began to laugh.

"No," he said, "I hadn't thought of it before. I don't go in for that stuff, much. But now that you mentioned it—it is an idea."

HE HELD the gun in his left hand, puffed harder at the cigarette in his right hand. It glowed like Al's cigarette had done a few minutes before. Very casually he began to walk toward Fiddler.

"You know," he said, "I've always wondered if it wouldn't hurt pretty badly if you got a lighted cigarette stuck behind the ear. It is sort of tender there, isn't it Fiddler?"

Fiddler half turned his head and stammered.

"D-d-d-don't! I'll talk."

"Okay. Who's the big guy that beat you up last night?"

He took his cigarette and moved it a little closer to the back of Fiddler's head. As he did so, he spoke to the Key.

"If Fiddler moves his head again, or turns around let him have it right in the stomach. I'll take a chance on the bullet being dead before it gets to me."

Then, with the cigarette held between his fingers, he barely touched the edge of Fiddler's dark hair behind his ear with his little finger. Fiddler jumped.

"Don't, don't," he cried, "I'll talk. I'll tell you anything you want to know."

"Okay," said King removing his finger from the ear, "who's the big bird?"

"He's Gilson," stammered Fiddler.

"Just what I thought," said King. "He's the clerk that disappeared from the D.A.'s office. Where can I find him?"

"I don't know," Fiddler said. "How should I know? He came here, beat me up and took the records with him. I've got some of my men out hunting him now."

"Okay," said King, "that's what we want to know."

King was still behind the three. He reached into the left-hand pocket of the henchman called Tony and drew out the key to the door.

"Let's go," he said to the Key.

He grinned at the three glaring criminals, who still held their hands above their heads.

"We may see you later," he called back.

"Hey," rasped Fiddler, "do I get those records?"

King smiled.

"I imagine you'll see them before you get through," he said. "Just sit tight and wait here."

He opened the door, passed out in the hall, and motioned for the Key to exit ahead of him. Then he locked the door from the outside and tossed the key to the other end of the hall.

Next he took a piece of white chalk from his pocket and made a strange mark on the woodwork—a crescent and a small circle. The sign of the Secret 6.

"That'll let anybody know we're working on this job," he told the Key.

The elevator that had brought the Key up was still there. They stepped inside and closed the door, pushed the button for the main floor. As they went down King laughed.

"I hope Farnham won't be waiting up the rest of the day and all night for her boyfriend Billy. How did you get in?"

The Key grinned.

"Oh, the usual way. You know how it is. One word from me and these doors and locks on safes and things just open wide. It's a cinch."

"It must be," said King as they stopped at the lobby. He walked to a telephone booth, took a nickel from his pocket, and dropped it into the slot. Dialed the operator.

"Give me police headquarters at once."

In answer to a gruff sleepy voice that came to him from police headquarters, King said:

"Good afternoon, captain. Got any idea who this is?"

"What are you doing, trying to kid me?" the police officer asked.

"No," King chuckled, "but I will if you don't take my tip and work on it quickly. Send the wagon up to—West 56th Street. Have the boys block all entrances, then go up to Mark Fiddler's apartment and arrest Fiddler and two men. They're behind this blackmail threat that has been started."

"Yeah," said the police officer rather lazily, "and who are you?"

"I'm King of the Secret 6," he shot back.

"King of the Secret 6—" the police officer exploded, "jumping jehosophat, you got a lot of nerve calling us up. Never mind, we'll get you some day."

"You're wasting time," King snapped. "If you lose those three birds don't blame me."

He hung up the receiver and he and the Key left the building.

"Where do we go now?" demanded the Key.

"The District Attorney's office," King said. "I don't think they'll recognize me and I rather suspect we'll have some fun."

As the car shot out to Broadway and turned downtown. King realized that the Key was looking at him steadily.

"Gee," the ex-crook said, "for poking your head in the meat-grinders you certainly got any drove of pigs stopped that I ever saw. And I suppose when you get in a jam up at the D.A.'s office you'll expect me to come up and help you there."

"No," King told him, "I don't think that will be necessary. If I can figure out some excuse for asking questions without arousing suspicion, there will be no danger."

"How about being a collector?"

"Not bad. A collector trying to find Mr. Henry Gilson. That ought to be hot. Especially three weeks after he's disappeared and all the police in seven counties are looking for him."

"That would be alright," said the Key.

"Lots of guys don't read the papers much. Besides, you can look dumb."

"Thanks," grinned King, "I wasn't sure. That gives me all kinds of confidence now."

Minutes later they pulled up before the District Attorney's office. King parked the car directly in front of the door regardless of the parking sign. As he climbed out he said to the Key,

"You stay right here behind the wheel. I might want to get out in a hurry."

HE WALKED up the steps and into the building. The words—DISTRICT ATTORNEY'S OFFICE—were written plainly across a glass door. He entered a large waiting room with benches around all four sides. Half-dozen people were sitting there.

He glanced at them, and then strode past into an office. A man looked at him from under spectacles. A man who had the look of years of service in the department. King cleared his throat nervously, reached in his inside coat pocket for several papers. He took them out and glanced on the back of one as though he were looking for a name to refresh his memory.

"I'm looking," he said, "for a man by the name of Henry Gilson that works here."

The man clerk stared at him. And with a touch of old Ireland in his voice he said: "You're looking for him? And I suppose you're the only one looking for him?"

"Oh," King said blankly. "Has he stepped out or gone for the day or something?"

"Holy Mackerel!" exploded the other one, "you don't read the papers, do you?"

"Not very much," said King. "My work with the collection agency keeps me pretty busy."

"Well I should think," retorted the other, "if you ain't read anything of Henry Gilson's disappearance. It was in all the papers." His eyes narrowed. "You mean to tell me that you ain't read nothing about Gilson disappearing?"

King tried to look embarrassed as he smiled.

"I'm afraid," he said, "I don't keep up on everything too well. You see my work—he's gone away then?"

"I'll say he's gone away," said the other.

"Er—could you tell me—what I mean to say is ah—er—could you give me directions where he lives? Or maybe a description of what Mr. Gilson looks like so I could be on the look-out for him?"

That seemed to take the other by surprise and before he thought he answered.

"Why sure," he said, "I can give you a description of him. He is a little fellow about five feet six and don't weigh over 120 pounds wringing wet so he—say, who the devil do you think you are? Think you can find him when the whole police force is looking for him?"

King tried to show embarrassment again.

"Well," he said, "of course I don't go so far as to think I could find him if the police couldn't. However I thought it might be possible that I might run into him. You wouldn't have a picture of him anywhere about, would you?"

The other swung around in his desk chair and pointed to a group photo, yellowed with age, hanging on the wall.

"That's the only picture we have that I know of," he said, "you'll see Gilson standing at the end of the group. He's a little fellow about as big as a pint of cider. See the fellow on the left that looks as if he might be the water boy to a baseball team?

Well, that's him and there ain't anybody in this office that's been able to figure out why he'd—"

His expression changed suddenly as a new idea came to him.

"Say," he exclaimed suddenly, "maybe the bill you're trying to collect would give us a line on where we might find him. Now you wait just a minute and I'll get one of the assistant district attorneys. I think he'd like to talk to you."

King hesitated.

"Perhaps he's busy now. I don't want to trouble him. Suppose I take a seat out in the waiting room."

At that moment a burly cop came puffing in with a cry:

"I just got word that the devil who calls himself King, that leader of the Secret 6, is running round loose. He 'phoned—told us to arrest Mark Fiddler in his apartment. The word was sent out and the boys get up there and there ain't anybody in the apartment and the door's locked. They busted down the door and find out that the place is empty. I guess they must have gone out a fire escape or something."

"You don't tell me," exclaimed the clerk, "so the Secret 6 is in on this job now. I'll say there's going to be the devil to pay."

"I'll say there is," returned the cop. "The old man's as mad as a wet hen. They'll be making monkeys out of us. They've done it already. How do we know that Mark Fiddler and his men were in that apartment when King called?"

All this time King was edging for the door. The clerk interrupted suddenly.

"Wait a minute until I take care of this matter." He turned to King. "I'll find out if the assistant District Attorney will see you."

King nodded. Almost bowed. "Thank you," he said. "I'll wait." He saw the cop look at him sharply.

CHAPTER 6
TWO GIANTS

THOSE KEEN eyes of the cop as they burned at him from across the room seemed to peer into his very thoughts. But King knew that was not so. For the make-up Shakespeare had applied disguised him quite well. Besides, the cops wouldn't expect him to be in the District Attorney's office of his own free will. He tried to act very calm as he moved toward the door. The cop seemed to be watching him steadily. Then he suddenly turned and looked out of the window. His glance had merely been one of curiosity.

King stepped out into the waiting room, turned to the right and moved back, casting a glance out of the tail of his eye toward the cop. But the officer wasn't watching.

Instantly King stepped to the outer door and out into the hall. It wouldn't do to run. Anyone running out of the District Attorney's office would be instantly suspected. So he walked. Walked with as much speed and as much calm as was possible with his nerves tingling as they were. Tingling not so much because of fear or suspense as with the news that he had just gained.

He pushed through the outer door into the street. As the portal swung shut slowly behind him he heard very faintly a voice yelling through the corridor.

"Hey, where the devil did that collector go?"

He ran at top speed now down the steps toward the roadster. The Key had the door open, the engine turning over. He leaped into the seat, half turned his head. The engine purred and the car shot down the street.

"They spot you?" the Key asked hurriedly.

King didn't answer directly. "Turn right then left then right then right again," he said hastily. "That ought to throw them off the track."

When they had made the first right turn, he peered back and saw that no cars seemed to be following. He settled down with a sigh of relief.

"They almost got me in a tight spot but only as a bill collector. They haven't the slightest idea who I really am."

He laughed.

"I thought that cop who came in was going to hold me. It would be funny to see his face if someone told him that he was within an arm's length of King of the Secret 6."

"Yeah," growled the Key, "that would have been hot."

"A lot hotter than you think," King said. "While I was standing there and getting a description of our friend, Henry Gilson, this cop came tearing in with news that I'd called up headquarters from Mark Fiddler's apartment house."

The Key's eyes brightened.

"Did they get Fiddler and those two mugs?" he asked.

"No," said King, "missed them cold. The three must have escaped by way of the fire-escape or something. Funny part of it is the police seem to think that I played a joke on them."

"Dumb clucks," the Key snapped.

King grinned.

"Oh, I don't know. Looks as if we are not much brighter in solving this mystery. Every clue seems to kill another clue."

"You're doin' O.K., King. Do you think the tall man was Gilson?"

King shook his head.

"It couldn't be," he said.

"Why?" the Key demanded. "Ain't Gilson a big guy?"

"I should say not," King laughed, "not unless the men that group picture of the D.A.'s staff were all giants. Henry Gilson stood on the end and looked like the water boy of a baseball team. The old fellow that I talked to said he was about five feet six, but I'd say he was closer to five feet five."

"Holy gee," the Key exploded, "you mean that he is a little whiffet of a guy? Now what do we do?"

KING WAS thoughtful for several minutes. They had turned uptown and were rolling on with the traffic.

"I'm beginning to wonder," he mused, "whether this big man that Patrolman Kelly saw leaving Mann's place really has any connection with the one who beat up Mark Fiddler."

"Holy gee," Key exploded, "that's like a guy wondering if the Empire State Building is still there just because he can't see it through the snow." He pointed to the great building as they passed it.

King nodded. "That's true. But if the guy wanted to be sure he would probably go close enough to see it—just to be confident of his own direction, you know. By the same line of reasoning, these two big men might not be the same person. New York is a big city and plenty of things can happen in it."

"Well for the love of Mike," the Key exploded, "what more do you want to know?"

"Two things. Flo tells me the fellow was close to seven feet tall."

"Yeah," countered the Key, "and Kelly said that the guy coming out of Mann's place was over six feet, didn't he?"

King nodded. "But there's a lot of difference between a man who is six feet, and another who is seven. There's where the argument comes in."

"So what?" said the Key.

"Oh, nothing serious," King answered, "only I think our next move will be to dig up Officer Kelly and talk to him personally."

"There you go," said the Key, "putting your head in the lion's mouth again."

"This isn't going to be so bad," King said. "I'll say I'm a special investigator or something."

"And I suppose you'll just look him up in the telephone directory to find out where he lives, him being the only Kelly in the book."

"No, I've got a better way than that. What's the paper you showed me the story in? The *Press?* Pull up in front of a drug store and I'll see what I can do."

The Key obeyed. He stopped before a drug store on a cross downtown street and King got out, went into a telephone booth. He dialed the number of the *Press* editorial room.

"Evening Press," sang out a girl's voice.

King broke into a smooth Irish dialect.

"I'm after wondering if you can give me the address of a relative of mine. I came in from Chicago last night and got ahold of your paper. I see the name of Patrolman Kelly. Now I remembered that I had a cousin here by the name of Kelly that was a cop. I ain't see him in a long time and—"

"Just a minute," said the girl, "I'll turn you over to someone in the editorial department."

A man's voice barked, "Hello," hurriedly.

"Hello yourself," said King, "this is Patrick Kelly from Chicago. I'm after getting in from Chicago last night and reading in your paper how a patrolman by the name of Michael Kelly got the lowdown on some suicide case. There was a Michael Kelly who was a cousin of mine. The last time I heard, he was one of the police force in New York and I ain't seen him in years and I was wondering if you could give me his address so I could look him up."

"Hold the line," barked the man on the other end.

There was a short intermission and then the man's voice came again. He mentioned an address in Brooklyn.

"I'm after thanking you from the bottom of my heart," King brogued.

He wrote the address down, went out to where the Key waited in the roadster.

"There she is," he said, handing him the address. "But it's past one. What say we stop somewhere and get a bite to eat? If Kelly is on the night shift, he may be sleeping. So we've got plenty of time."

They ate and talked and smoked. It was mid-afternoon when they pulled up before the Brooklyn address. The Kelly's lived in a drab stone apartment building. Children played about the entrance. King asked one of them:

"Any of you kids know where Patrolman Kelly lives?"

"Sure," said one, "this is his boy here. Mike, show the man where your old man lives."

Young Michael was a freckled-faced, stocky built youngster with a genial grin.

"Sure mister," he said, "I'll show you. Are you a reporter from the papers?"

King hesitated then he shook his head.

"No sonny," he said, "I'm in a similar position but not with the newspapers. I write stories for magazines and I thought if I could talk with your father about this case I might get an idea."

"Gee," said the kid. "Come on. I'll show you."

He led the way up two flights of stairs and burst into a door.

"Hey Pop," he yelled, "here's a man that writes stories. He thinks maybe he can write a story about the Mann case."

A big fellow came into the living room. He seemed to almost make the doorway bulge as he stood there. He was in his under-shirt and trousers with the suspenders hanging down from the waist. One side of his face was well lathered; he had evidently been in the process of shaving.

"Oh a story writer," he said.

HE CAME forward, held out his hand and King took it. As he moved King noticed that the head of Michael Kelly came surprisingly close to the top of the door casing. There was possibly seven or seven and one-half inches between his head and the top, certainly not any more than that. Patrolman Kelly was a big man.

"So you're a story writer," Kelly went on. "That's a good occupation. I ain't never met any fellows in your business before except one and he was a writer fellow from England. Sir Somebody or Other who used to write detective stories. It was over to a banquet I was sent to sort of handle the situation and I was sitting just as close to him as I am to you now. I used to read his stories, too, afterwards. Boy, that fellow could make your blood run cold."

"I'm afraid you won't find me near as famous a writer as this Englishman you mention," King smiled.

"Well, you're a likely looking young fellow anyway," said the cop. "What might your name be? Maybe I read some of your stories. Do you write westerns? That's the kind I read."

"I'm sorry," King said, "but I only go in for the detective stuff."

"Well, that's too bad now," the cop said, "but anyway if you'll tell me your name I'll get hold of some of your detective stuff and read it. Sure I will."

King mentioned a name that was most familiar to him. But it didn't seem particularly familiar to Patrolman Michael Kelly, although he widened his eyes and nodded his head.

"Shure, shure, I've heard of you. I think I've read some of your stuff. And you want to put this Mann case into a detective story, do you?"

"I thought if I could ask you some questions," King said, "I might find something that would be usable."

"Shure and I'll be glad to tell you," Kelly agreed. "Anything you want, but I don't read detective stories very much. It gives me a pain in the neck the way you fellows have a newspaper reporter or somebody solve the crime. You make us cops look like dummies."

King laughed.

"That's just some writers. In my stories I always try to have a detective on the force put it over. The way it should be."

"Shure," said the cop, "I'm certainly glad to hear that. What did you say your name was?"

King mentioned the name again.

"Shure, shure," said the cop, "I'll remember that and get something with your stuff in. And now what was it you wanted to know?"

"It was regarding this Mann suicide," King explained. "I got your address from *The Press* and thought I'd run up after you'd had a chance to sleep."

"Now that was a funny thing," said the cop. "This fellow Horace Mann. He's got all the money in the world. He don't have to worry about nothing and then what does he do but shoot himself. I'm telling you it's hard to figure out people sometimes. Course the boys in the department are figuring out its blackmail. There were old records stolen out of the District Attorney's office about three weeks ago. And there was something in him about a deal Mann was mixed up in years ago. About midnight I was walking my beat and the door of the mansion opens just as I was going by on the other side of the street and out comes a big man. A big fellow he was. I couldn't see him very plain 'cause it was dark, and a big dog followed him. Big as a horse the dog was and when I shot the dog the big fellow runs and me after him but he gets away. I went back and looked at the dog. He was like them we'd killed earlier. I called headquarters and they came and got the giant beast and then I went on walkin' my beat again. I was just walking by Mann's place an hour later when the butler comes tearing out hollering for the police. I ran up and he tells me his Master has just shot himself. So I go in and take a look at him and he is laying back in his chair with a hole in his head and the gun on the floor where he had dropped it out of his hand."

King nodded.

"That ought to make the basis of a fine story," he said.

"You think so?" the cop asked, widening his eyes. "I could give you plenty of things like that, except, of course, for the big dog. Something like that happens to the boys every day or so."

"What I mean," King said, "it ought to make a good story because of the big dog and all. Just how big was the man?"

Patrolman Michael Kelly hesitated.

"Over six feet," he said at last. Then he stopped and his eyes narrowed in deep thought. "Yeah, he was a big fellow. Like I told the papers."

"As big as you are?" King asked.

"Well now, I'd say so. If anything, bigger than I am."

"How much bigger?" King asked.

"Well now of course," Kelly answered, "I wasn't standing right next to him, but I should say he was maybe two or three inches taller than I am. I'm six feet in my stocking feet. Course these big shoes we wear on the beat, they've got heavy soles and heels and they set me up some. That would make me a good six feet-one anyway."

"And you'd say," King countered, "that this man was perhaps two or three inches taller than you?"

"Yeah, just about. Say, I just happened to think of something."

"What's that?" King asked instantly.

"There was one thing that might help the boys hunt him. Did you ever see a farmer from out of the back woods come down to the Big City in a mail-order suit of clothes? Well, that's the way he impressed me."

"Why?"

"Most everything about him," said Kelly. "He walked with a long stride like he was used to covering plenty of ground. Had sort of an important swing too, come to think about it. And then his clothes didn't seem to fit him."

"Were they too small or too large?" King asked.

"A mite too small for him," the cop said. "His arms and legs kind of stuck out like he ordered the suit small because he had measured himself wrong."

"That is strange," King commented.

"Maybe you can use that in your story," Kelly said. "I got to hurry with my shaving now so that I can be down to headquarters in time to go on my beat at four o'clock."

"Of course," King said. "I don't want to bother you anymore but could you tell me what the servants in the Mann house said about this fellow?"

"Nobody saw him except the butler and Horace Mann

himself," said the cop. "And the butler was so upset he couldn't think of anything. All he remembered was that he came, rang the bell and insisted on seeing Mr. Mann. The butler thought he was a country cousin or something and Mann said to let him in. That's all he knows."

"I see," said King, "well I'll leave you now to get ready. Thanks very much."

CHAPTER 7
DEATH TRAIL

KING TURNED and went out of the apartment. Young Mike Kelly went with him, walking beside him with a rather worshipful gaze.

"Gee mister," he said, "I never collected autographs before but I'm going to start now with yours."

"Sure," said King, "I have a pencil. Have you got a piece of paper?"

The kid nodded.

"Right here," he said, taking a torn piece of paper out of his pocket. "You can write your name on the back of this grocery slip."

King wrote his name—or rather the name of the author he had mentioned to the cop.

"Thanks mister," the kid said grinning happily. "Boy, I'm going to get autographs from everybody now. I mean all of the big shots like you and maybe someday I'll even get the autograph of the president of the United States."

King laughed.

"Better than that," he said as they reached the sidewalk, "maybe you'll get to be president of the United States someday."

"I'd rather be mayor of New York," the kid said.

King waved goodbye and stepped into the car. He was chuckling as the Key drove away from the curb.

"Where to now," the Key asked.

"Just stop anywhere by a 'phone and let me call Flo," King said. "I want to ask her a question. Kelly told me something no one else mentioned. It seems that this big bird that left the banker's mansion looked like a farmer come to town with a mail-order suit that was too small for him."

"Gee that is something," said Key. "Just a big hay-kicker all dressed up in his Sunday Shears & Sawbuck sent-to-measure suit."

"I'm almost beginning to think," King decided, "that we're getting two men mixed up. This cop is a good six feet and he said that the big bird was no more than three inches taller."

The Key's eyes narrowed as they left the street ahead of them for a moment and shot to King's face. "A guy only six feet three or four wouldn't have to duck through a door that was six feet eight."

"That's what I'd like to know," King said gravely, "and that's what makes me believe that the two men are not the same."

"Holy Gee," the Key exclaimed, "that's right."

He pulled up in front of a drug store. "Here's your telephone."

"Thanks," said King, "I'm going to call Flo and see if she can throw any more light on this."

There was a wait of a few minutes before Flo's musical voice came over the wires to him.

"Flo, this is King. I wanted to check up on one or two things."

"Of course," said Flo, "anything I can tell you, King."

"You said," he went on, "that this big man had to stoop to get out of the door of Mark Fiddler's room? You're sure?"

"Absolutely. I remember it very clearly. You went to Fiddler's?"

"Yes. Quite a while ago."

"Did you have any trouble," she asked. "A little," King replied, "but the Key got there just in time. About this big bird. Was there anything peculiar about him—his clothes, for instance?" King questioned.

"Come to think about it," Flo said slowly, "he did look rather odd. He walked with a long stride and his clothes seemed too small for him."

"Thanks Flo, that's what I wanted to know. Your description tallies with the man Kelly saw leaving Horace Mann's house except that he is eight or ten inches taller."

Flo laughed. "Maybe the one we saw was the big brother of the other one."

"Maybe," agreed King joining her in the laugh.

"Or maybe," she said, "this fellow had shrunk eight or ten inches when I saw him."

"Sure," laughed King, "and maybe horses will be flying by tomorrow. No, I'm afraid we've got two entirely different men, and that we're on a wild goose chase. At any rate I'll keep you posted, and don't hesitate to let us know if you pick up anything."

"I certainly won't," she said.

The receivers clicked and King was on his way back to the car. He shook his head and his face carried a baffled look as he climbed back into the roadster.

"Find out anything?" the Key said.

"Yes," said King, "almost too much. It looks to me as if we are chasing the same guy only he is twins with one of the twins eight or ten inches taller."

He told the Key what he had learned. The Key's eyes widened.

"Holy Gee," he said, "that's a dumb thing, isn't it. Here we got two guys supposed to be the same person only one is eight or ten inches taller than the other.

They're both mixed up in the same deal. They've both got clothes that don't fit them. They both walk with great long strides."

"Yes," said King, "and they'd both be the same person except that one's taller than the other."

"Well," the Key shrugged, "where do we go from here?"

"I think we might as well beat it back to the shack," King said. "There might be some news there."

THE CAR turned out on the main North Long Island highway and picked up speed. King was silent during almost the entire trip. He came to the west end of the woods in which the cabin was hidden.

"Nothing coming in front," said the Key. "How are we behind?"

"Wait a minute," King said, "there's a car coming behind."

The Key whirled in his seat and glanced back.

"Holy Gee!" he exploded. "I've seen that car before. It has been trailing us, I think."

King turned, studied the vehicle. "Step on it," he said quickly. "We can't turn into the bed rock drive with that car in sight. If it's someone who is watching us we've got to keep him guessing."

The Key hesitated then he spoke to King.

"Here you take the wheel. I'm not so hot when it comes to this fast driving."

As he spoke he slid over into the seat. King pulled himself up and got hold of the wheel, then slammed the foot accelerator down to the floor. The roadster shot ahead. The Key had turned and was watching through the rear glass of the top.

"They're speeding up," he said. "We've got to lose them if we're going to get anywhere and that car they've got isn't going to be any cinch to lose either. Those sedans may be small but they can go like the dev—like everything."

King was watching the road. His eyes shifted back and forth to the speedometer. The roadster was doing 60—65—70—75—80.

"You doing top now?" the Key asked.

"Almost," King replied. "I think she'll do pretty nearly 90. We'll find out before we get through."

The speedometer was sneaking up toward 85.

"I think they've dropped back a little bit," the Key said.

"Good," said King. "There's a dirt road up ahead and it's pretty dusty, I think maybe we can plaster them with dust. That may hold them up a while."

He slapped on the brakes. Tires squealed. Then the roadster lurched into the dirt road.

"Boy look at that bus come," the Key exclaimed. "There's three men in it. I can see all three heads sticking up looking out of the windshield. One guy in the back seat and two in front. They're slowing up to take the turn now."

"And here's where we plaster them with more dust than they've seen in a long time."

"Right," said the Key, "here's mud in your eyes, you mugs."

The roadster was now hurling at top speed on the dirt road. A terrific cloud of dust streamed out behind them. A cloud of dust that spread out to the fields on either side and hid the pursuing car completely from view.

"Wonder who it might be?" the Key asked.

"It might be one of two persons," said King. "Either the cops or Fiddler and his men."

"Then it's Fiddler," said the Key definitely. "Cause if it was the cops they'd get out and find out what's going on."

"I think you're right," King decided, "and if it's Fiddler he's trailing us to find our hideout. He thinks I know where those old records are. Can you see the car now?"

"Nothing," said the Key, "but I'll bet they're coming. Boy—

The musical noice of Flo came
to him over the 'phone.

how they can see far enough ahead to drive without hitting something on this road is enough to make a guy get the jitters."

The roadster careened about curves. Gravel flew with the dust now. They sped on and on. Then down ahead King saw a state highway leading to right and left. He slapped on his brakes, spun the wheel and the roadster zipped around the corner. On down that road they sped. There was no dust flying behind them now. The Key had turned around in his seat and was staring constantly out of the rear window.

Suddenly he exclaimed: "Here they come!"

The roadster was doing 75 now, having picked up speed after making the turn.

"They can't make it! They can't make it!" the Key yelled excitedly. "They just slammed out of the dust that we threw in their faces and they didn't know they were hitting a cross road. They'll try to make the turn and come after us. There goes the car down on one side. They're going into the ditch!"

King was watching in the mirror. He saw everything that the Key described—saw the car come shooting out of the dirt road under a cloud of dust—saw it lurch to one side as it tried to slow down for the turn. Saw it shoot off a little embankment, crash and turn over.

"That was sure luck," King exclaimed fervently. He hesitated. "I wonder if we ought to go back."

"Hell," returned the Key, "I mean goodness. That wasn't luck. You planned it just that way, you mug. Don't try to kid me. And darn clever work too. Don't kid yourself, we're not going back. I suppose you'll cry your eyes out if Fiddler and those two guys that were burning you with a cigarette would get killed in an automobile accident. You're the craziest guy!"

King sped on.

"I suppose you're right about not stopping. Of course we don't know, for sure, if it is Fiddler's gang. But I can't figure out who else it might be. And after all one can't help feeling sorry for anyone in a car crash, King." There was a twinkle in his eye. BUT HE drove on. Swung into a road that turned on to another and connected with the main highway on the north shore of Long Island. And with no one in sight in either direction he turned on the bed rock secret road that led to their hideout. They reached the place where the cars were hidden in the brush and King drove the roadster up beside the sedan.

"Well," he said as they walked toward the cabin, "I wonder what's happened while we've been gone?"

The Key shrugged.

"I'd like to hear some—news that would clear up this business of the twin giants," he said.

Just before they reached the cabin they met the Bishop and Shakespeare taking a walk. Shakespeare struck a pose, lifting his hand palm outward like an Indian in salute.

"Hail, gallant chief of our little band, to our jungle hideaway," he boomed.

The Key grinned.

"The hail you say," he laughed. "Check that one Bishop."

The Bishop's eyes twinkled.

"What goes," he asked. "We heard that you have been at work."

The four walked back together to the cabin.

"You've heard?" King asked.

"Yes," said the Bishop. "The Dummy gave us a report. It seemed that this morning a gentleman by the name of King who purported to be the leader of the Secret 6, called the police and told them to go to the apartment of Mark Fiddler and arrest him and two of his men. They think that it was merely a joke for when they went there Mark Fiddler and his men were gone."

King smiled.

"Yes," he said, "I did call up the police. I'll tell you all about it when we get together."

Luga put in an appearance around the corner of the cabin.

"Luga glad to see you back, master," he said. "Luga worry about you."

"That's nice of you," King said.

They entered and found the Doctor working with some of his laboratory equipment.

"Well," he said, "what's this we hear about the leader of our loyal band kidding the police?"

King took his coat off, sat down and lighted a cigarette.

"I'll start at the beginning and try to tell you everything that's happened. Then I think you'll understand much more readily."

King began at the time they had left the cabin. He told of his visit to Flo's apartment, what he had learned there, and of his subsequent visits to Mark Fiddler, the office of the District Attorney and the home of Patrolman Michael Kelly.

"It seems," he said, "that this trip of mine has served to ball things up in general."

"I told you it was a wild goose chase in the first place," the Doctor reminded him.

"I wouldn't say that," King countered. "It is really getting pretty interesting even though it is hard to understand. Let's review the facts. Mann was in a position to be blackmailed. A tall man—not over six feet three inches—was seen to leave his house shortly before he committed suicide.

"Flo and her friend, on the other hand, saw a big man leave Fiddler's apartment with a bundle under his arm. But that man was about seven feet tall. So it doesn't seem as though they could possibly be the same person."

The Doctor laughed rather harshly. "I suppose," he said, "you're going to try to make us believe that they are twins, only one guy is eight or ten inches taller."

King's eyes snapped.

"I think Doctor," he said, "we'll all get along a great deal better if you take this situation seriously instead of as a joke. From what I've learned today Mark Fiddler is no weakling and it certainly was a giant who beat him up. Mark knows that this big fellow has the stolen records and he knows what those records contain. He's out and he's on the loose with those papers. He's a dangerous individual and don't make any mistake about that. There's no telling where his blackmail racket might end."

The Doctor grunted and lighted a cigarette. The Bishop sat back in his chair, filled his Meerschaum pipe. He lighted it and blew great clouds of smoke into which he stared with dreamy thoughtful eyes before turning slowly to King. There was a twinkle in his eye.

"It makes rather a baffling situation, doesn't it?" he said.

"It certainly does Bishop," King admitted. "Here we develop a perfectly good case against the big man that is perhaps six feet two or—three inches tall. It gets to the point where it seems as though we only have to move for this one big man when we find that he's twins except that he isn't because one of the twins is eight or ten inches taller than the other."

"And yet," the Bishop said, "you just told us that this Mr. Fiddler confessed that the big man who beat him up was Gilson."

"That's what stumps all of us," King said. "The only way I can figure it out is that Fiddler must have lied about who the big fellow was."

"Say listen here," the Key said, "I got an idea. Suppose Fiddler tried to get Gilson to steal the records and he refused. Suppose then he hired this big man to get 'em and nab Gilson in the bargain to turn suspicion on the little runt."

"Say," King said, "maybe you've guessed something at that. Let's go on a little farther with that. Say they bumped Gilson off and hid the body or else they're keeping him in some safe place where he can't get away. Then let's carry the story a little farther and suppose that Fiddler and this giant bird get in an argument and the big bird beats up Fiddler and walks off with the records."

"Say," cried the Doctor suddenly interested, "that doesn't sound so bad now that you've put it that way."

"Of course not," said King.

"But then," suggested the Doctor, "who is the man seen by Patrolman Kelly?"

King shrugged.

"It seems, Doctor," he said, "that except for a mere difference of eight or ten inches the whole story hangs together very nicely."

"It does," agreed the Doctor. "Fiddler sent this big fellow over to Horace Mann's place to tell him what would happen if he didn't pay. The next thing Fiddler hears is that Mann has committed suicide. When the big guy tries to collect his money from Fiddler he says nothing doing, so the big fellow beats him up, takes the records and walks out. It looks to me like it is a perfectly open and shut proposition there."

"Yes," King smiled, "except for the eight-or ten inches difference in height. If we had that accounted for we'd—"

Suddenly a whistling sound came out of the short-wave receiver and a monotonous voice became audible and took shape. "Pipe down," hissed the Key, "it's the Dummy again. Maybe he's got some dope for us."

CHAPTER 8
THE UNEARTHLY FOOTPRINTS

THE VOICE came clearly. They could distinguish words. Words of the Dummy.

"Hello, Secret 6. Hello, Secret 6. This is the Dummy. Police are still awful mad about King calling them up and telling them to go and arrest Mark Fiddler and a couple of his men. They're working on another job in this case now. They got wind of the fact that a blackmail job was started at some rich guy's house on Long Island but they can't figure out who it is. Somebody dropped a tip that a blackmail job was being pulled off and that's all they know. They don't know the victim and they're trying to find out now. Anyway, they got the card this afternoon. The post-card said: 'Arrest Mark Fiddler before he has time to blackmail a certain wealthy man on Long Island. Signed, the Giant.' The police were thinking that one of you guys of the Secret 6 sent this for a joke or they think that King was right about Mark Fiddler needing arresting. Anyway they're looking for him and they're trying to find out who the rich guy is on Long Island that's going to get it. You got that?"

King nodded.

"That complicates things and makes them clearer again at the same time. Apparently we are back where we started except that we know somebody else has either been blackmailed or will be very shortly."

"Yes," beamed the Bishop, "except for the slight discrepancy of eight or ten inches. For a while it would at least have looked a little clearer if we hadn't known about that Horace Mann case. The eight or ten inches wouldn't bother us a particle if we knew exactly what we know now. We'd know that there was a little competition in the blackmail business going on with the giant handling one side and Mark Fiddler handling the other. What I'd like to know is who on Long Island is in the process of being blackmailed."

"By George," the Doctor said, "I wish we had duplicate radio sets for your friends, Key, so that we could talk back and forth to them and tell them when we want certain information. I believe

I'll make some up so we can converse on the same short wave they talk to us on."

Suddenly another whistling humming sound came from the shortwave receiver.

"Wait a minute," said the Key. "These friends of mine ain't so dumb as they might be. They'll shoot us all the dope they can get on the case as fast as they can get it. Keep your shirt on and maybe you won't have to make those sets for a while. Here's somebody coming in to shoot us some dope right now."

Out of the radio came a voice: "Hello Secret 6. Hello Secret 6."

"Shhhh," hissed the Key, "it's Legs Larkin, listen."

"Hello Secret 6," the voice continued. "Legs Larkin talking, I got some dope on a blackmail racket. My daughter works for J. Lawrence Pennington and his wife on their estate up near Glen Cove. She is first maid there and she just came home and told me that Pennington is all worked up about some blackmail proposition. It seems there was a card left last night at his house saying he'd be killed if he told the police; it ordered him to send all servants away too. That's why my daughter came home. She said the chauffeur and the butler started on an investigation on their own hook and that they found huge footsteps in the flowerbed out in the front. Some great big guy must have left that card. She said Pennington is scared green. The note was signed 'The Giant' and it said he would be back tonight to collect. Thought maybe you would like to know. So long. This is Legs Larkin."

THE RADIO hummed for a moment, then fell silent. The

six men inside of the cabin sat motionless staring at each other. King was the first to speak.

"It looks," he said, "as though we have a job on our hands, don't you think, Doctor?"

The Doctor nodded. "It most certainly does," he said. "I confess at first I was skeptical but now that this giant seems to be coming more and more into prominence it certainly is taking on an aspect of great interest."

King glanced out of the window.

"I think," he said, "we've just got time to eat a bite of supper and then hop into the car and land over there after dark. Do any of you know where J. Lawrence Pennington's estate is at Glen Cove?"

"I believe I can point the way," Shakespeare said. "I've known those estates quite well."

"Good," King said.

He got up. "Come on, Luga," he said, "I'll help you wrestle some grub for them, and then we'll be on our way."

"You'll take me too, master?" Luga asked eagerly.

"You're right, big boy," King smiled. "It's dark now and you're not apt to be recognized or throw suspicion on the rest of us, and I won't be a bit surprised to see a real fight that you can take part in too, Luga."

Luga took on more life with that news. He hurriedly got a meal together for the men with King's help. They ate hurriedly, talked little and spent no time to smoke afterward. Then King led the gang through the forest as dusk settled.

When they reached the sedan they all climbed into it and

King backed it out of its hiding place. They drove out of the bed rock drive and turned on the highway.

"I'm just wondering," he said, "how this thing works out."

"We're all wondering that," said the Bishop. "But to just exactly what do you refer?"

King smiled.

"Let's wait until we get there and we'll see what the lay out is," he said. "Then if I'm wrong there's no use of the rest of us getting excited about it."

They passed through Oyster Bay, down through the tree covered lanes and drives in the dark row. Passed the great estates of that section and then to Glen Cove.

"I believe," said the Shakespeare, "you turn right at the next road. That ought to take us down to the Sound and the estates."

King turned. He passed a great walled estate and then another one quite similar to it.

"It's the next one to it, I believe," Shakespeare said.

King inspected it as they drove by.

"Yes," he said, "that's the Pennington estate."

This estate was not walled like the others. Rather it was merely encircled by a thick, well-kept box hedge that was fence-like in its appearance. They could see it although it was practically dark. King drove past the entrance. Drove on to where the road turned to the left to skirt the Sound a little way. There, in a darker spot under some low-hanging trees, he left the car.

"Now listen," he said, "we're all well-armed but don't take any chances of killing the wrong man. We may not get any action at all tonight but at least we'll have more of an idea of what's up over here than we had. I want to go in and have a talk with Mr. Pennington himself if he is in and I rather imagine he will be. He probably is too scared to leave the place, poor fellow. He must be about frantic. It'll probably be best if the rest of you park yourself somewhere about the house in clumps of shrubbery here and there so that you can see anybody who goes in or out of the house without being seen."

They crawled through the hedge at the end of the estate. The property was well shrubbed with neatly kept bushes and trees. Here and there in the dim light they could see a flower bed that adorned the great expanse of lawn. They spread out and approached the house moving from tree to shrub. King was out in front.

"Everybody down," he said, "let's wait a little and see if anything turns up, then we can go on."

They crouched there in the darkness and waited fifteen—twenty minutes.

"Fine," King commented, "I think it is clear now. I'll go up and see if I can get Pennington to talk."

He kept on moving in the deep shadows and reached the front door, walking softly up the steps. He rang the bell several times. Then he heard footsteps in the hall beyond. There were no lights in the lower floor of the house. He saw the curtains at the window close to the door move slightly. A half minute later the door opened—opened three or four inches. A lock chain kept it from opening farther.

The white face of a man peered at him in the darkness. Neither stood in the light.

"I'm ready to talk," said the man in a shaky voice. "What do you want?"

"Please don't be alarmed," King said, "we're here to help you. We're not the blackmailers. If you'll open the door and let me in I can explain. But it wouldn't be well for the blackmailers to come and find us talking here."

"I'll do all my talking through this crack of the door," the man said, making sure that his body was behind it.

"Look," King said, "you don't understand. I'm King of the Secret 6 and the other five are outside scattered about your estate where they can watch the house. We've come to help you."

The man gasped.

"Why didn't you say so in the first place," he said.

He half closed the door so that he could unlock the chain. He opened the door wide. King stepped in. Instantly the man closed the door behind him.

"Now," the man demanded, "the first thing I want to know is how did you find out about this?"

They were standing in the dark hall.

"You're Mr. Pennington, aren't you?" King asked.

"Yes," said the other, "and you actually mean you're King of the Secret 6."

King bowed in the darkness.

"At your service sir," he declared. "Can we have a place where we can turn on the light and see each other? I'm sure it would help us both if we could."

"Yes," said the man more easily, "come in to my den. It's thoroughly shuttered.

79

That was where I was when the bell rang. I'll tell you frankly, Mr. King, I'm almost frantic with the suspense of this thing."

"Just King will do," he said. "And I don't blame you for feeling pretty nervous about it."

PENNINGTON LED him down the hall and into a small room closing the door after him. A table light glowed and King could see that the one large window of the room was tightly shuttered. Now he saw Mr. Pennington clearly.

He had the look of a prosperous business man. He had keen eyes, a close-cropped gray moustache and an open honest face. He was rather plump in build.

"I imagine," King said, "these blackmailers think they have something pretty bad on you."

Pennington cleared his throat. His face whitened a little more.

"They not only think they have something pretty bad—they have. It would not go so well with me if it were to reach the papers. You see I have been in the shipping business most of my life. Twenty years ago an accident happened to one of my ships. I say an accident but as a matter of fact it wasn't exactly that. It was—er—er—one of those preventable accidents."

He cleared his throat again nervously.

"You may understand King that in a business such as mine anything that will shake public or business confidence is apt to ruin one's business. An employee managed to weaken the boilers in one of my ships so that it blew up under the unusual strain. He swore when the investigation came up that he had insisted that the boilers were too weak and that he had told me and I had ordered him to go on with them like that. It was a lie. As a matter of fact he was the one who had been trusted to keep the machinery in tip-top shape and to replace anything as it was needed. That as I say, King, was twenty years ago. There were several lives lost in the explosion. It cost my company heavily. Then there was the suggestion that there might be dirt in the whole deal and the strange part of it was that about the time the authorities were considering taking this employee of mine and grill him on the subject, his body was found floating in the East River. I've always had a strange suspicion that the competing company was instrumental in causing his death when they heard that he was to testify, but as you can realize, the whole thing looked very black for me. However, I succeeded in living the thing down and today I'm in the passenger-carrying business to quite an extent. You can understand what it would mean to my business which hasn't been any too good in the last three years, if some of these yellow sheets and sensational newspapers revived the old story. I'm afraid they could ruin me and my business— as a matter of fact I'm sure of it. I would be much better off if I paid a blackmailer to keep him quiet. I hope you comprehend."

"Perfectly. More perhaps than you know. The record of this affair twenty years ago was set down in the old records of the District Attorney's office, Mr. Pennington?"

"Why yes, I presume so. I never thought of it but I suppose they have all those old records," said Pennington.

"Did you know," King asked, "that old records for quite a number of years had been stolen—as a matter of fact were stolen three weeks ago from the District Attorney's office?"

"Good Heavens no," shouted Pennington. Then he stopped.

"By Jove," he said, "come to think about it I do remember reading something about that in the paper.

"Surely you don't believe that that has anything to do with this—er—difficulty that I'm in now?"

"I believe," said King, "it has everything to do with it."

"What I'd like to know most," Pennington said, "is how you found out about this warning I received."

King studied him a moment.

"Mr. Pennington," he said, "you look to me like a very sensible sort of a man. I don't want to betray a trust and get someone in trouble but I believe that the one responsible for letting us know should be rewarded in some way. Particularly if we can do you some good."

"You mean," said Pennington not unkindly, "that someone of my household let the information slip out?"

"If I tell you," King asked, "you'll promise not to discharge this person?"

"Indeed I do," said Pennington emphatically. "As a matter of fact I'll raise her pay—I'll double it. By George that was a brilliant idea. You see I have been scared to tell the police because if I got the police in this they'd want to know what I was being blackmailed about. And it would be difficult to explain without starting this old story all over again. But I never thought of trying to bring you and your Secret 6 into the case. As a matter of fact if I had thought of it I'd not have known where to reach you."

"That's true," said King. "It does make it rather difficult, doesn't it? Well, it's a young woman in your employ by the name of Larkin, you know who I mean?"

"Of course, of course," said Pennington, "and a very fine young woman she is too. She is the first maid of our household. Is she the one?"

"I think so," King smiled. "If you raise her pay she'll be very much delighted."

"As good as done," said Pennington. "And now what can I do to help you? Remember anything I own is at your disposal, young man."

"I don't think it will take that much," King said. "First I'd like to see the note that was left under your door."

Pennington reached into his coat pocket. Drew out a folded sheet of paper.

"There it is," he said. "You may read it for yourself."

King took the sheet and scanned it.

Pennington:

Your business would be ruined if the Yellow Sheets got hold of the old story of the explosion twenty years ago. If you pay enough, I'll keep my mouth shut. Have all your servants leave the house at once. I'll kill you if you tell the police. Be there alone tonight. You'll be told how much money to pay and what to do with it.

The Giant.

King handed the paper back to Pennington.

"I understand," he said, "that your chauffeur and butler found some large foot prints out in the flower bed before they left. Is that correct?"

"Yes," Pennington replied.

King got up.

"I think our next move," he suggested, "is to look at those footprints. They're pretty large aren't they?"

Pennington nodded. Seemed to shudder as he did so.

"They're the prints of shoes," he said. "They are larger than any shoes I ever saw before."

"I'll have a look at them," King stated.

He started for the door and Pennington stopped him.

"I can't tell you, King," he said, "how relieved I am to know that you and your Secret 6 are working on this case."

"Thank you," acknowledged King. Then he was gone. Pennington called softly as he left.

"The steps—the footprints that we saw were in the flower bed, right out front of the porch, and some others are under the front door. Do you want me to go with you?"

"No," King replied, "I think you'd better stay inside as the orders said. I'll make it alright."

He trotted down the steps and strode to the flower bed in front of the porch. He was just about to turn the flash light on. Standing there in a crouched position he heard a low whistling sound from one of the bushes close at hand. It was the call of the night bird. He froze there in his tracks for an instant, did not move any. He heard very softly a rustling on the lawn and a few seconds later a voice.

"Master, master, this way. Crawl on ground."

King flattened to the ground. He began to wriggle to the place where the voice came from and as fast as he could. Then he reached out and the hand that met his was Luga's. The giant black had turned around and was crawling back toward some bushes. They reached the shelter of the bushes and crouched in the shadows.

"Master, somebody come while you gone."

"Who?" King hissed.

CHAPTER 9
MURDER BY PAIRS

KING'S VOICE sounded almost hollow in the stillness, yet he spoke in his lowest whisper. He peered out in the wide expanse of lawn. He strained his eyes to see something in the darkness. Couldn't make out a thing Luga was talking of.

"We just see shadow move in trees," Luga said. "Big shadow over there by entrance where driveway go out on street. You say not to shoot unless we sure who it is so we not shoot."

"That's right," King agreed. "Where are the rest of the men?"

"They around house behind different bush," Luga said. "They slip out around house when shadow of something comes."

"Do you mean," King demanded, "there is a shadow of something big over behind that hedge?"

"Yes," replied Luga, "it come like animal on all four feet or maybe like man on hands and knees. Very big. Can't see good. Just see shadow move when it stop. We not see any more."

King hesitated a moment. His brain was whirling—surely this was their chance—yet he couldn't be positive.

"Did this look like a great giant of a man? A lot bigger than you, Luga?"

"Yes, master, very big. He not stand up so we could see how tall but he crouched down. Big almost like giant bear when he crawl along—maybe bigger. He was bigger than the biggest gorilla Luga ever see in Africa."

"Boy, that could be big," King said. Again King tried his best to see through the darkness by the hedge that Luga said the giant lay. There was only a dull black lane in the darkness that surrounded them. For several minutes they lay there. Then King asked.

"Where did it come from—the giant, I mean?"

"Nobody know," Luga puzzled. "We just see him moving along hedge. He wait there now."

"I wonder," mused King, "what he can be waiting for. Do you think he has probably spotted anybody here on the lawn?"

"No master," answered Luga.

"But he is waiting for something," King persisted. "There isn't a move there beside the hedge. He is lying right there where he can jump up and grab them when they come in the drive. Maybe that whistle of yours made him suspicious."

"Luga whistle like night bird," said the big black man. "Giant over there he not move—Luga watch him."

"But it might have made him stop," King insisted.

"No, he come and stop two or three minutes before you come out of house. He no move when he hear you come either."

"Then," said King, "if he was here to go up and blackmail

Pennington he should have reached up and collared me, put me out of the way and come on with his business."

"Yes, master."

"By George," whispered King, "he's waiting for somebody. I'm convinced of that."

They waited a few minutes longer. King grew more and more restless.

"Luga," he queried. "What do you say we crawl out across the lawn after him? If he jumps us we can fill him full of lead."

"All right, master, you say shoot him?"

"Come to think about it, I don't know," said King. "He is a suspicious character, that's a cinch. But do we know positively that he is doing anything wrong? We may suspect that his going into the Horace Mann residence had something to do with the Horace Mann suicide but we haven't any way of knowing it positively. Yet at any rate he did go in and beat up Mark Fiddler and Fiddler admitted that he took the stolen records away from him. But that seems to me more to his credit than anything else. No, Luga, I don't think we can rush him and plug him full of holes on that much evidence. You've got to have more than that to kill a man."

Then suddenly he stopped short. They could hear a car purring down the road. It was slowing. They could see the lights gleaming through the hedge. Now suddenly the lights went out and the car continued to come on but moved slower and slower so that they could scarcely hear it now. Then they saw the shadow of it appear around the hedge. The car was turning in the driveway. King felt Luga's hand on his arm pressing in a signal.

"Look master," Luga hissed, "see shadow creeping out of hedge now. Giant going for car."

"Yes," King nodded, "I see it."

Then both men turned there in the shadows of the shrubs. A form like a gigantic gorilla raced out from behind that hedge. The car was still in motion after it turned the driveway. It was moving past them and the hedge at perhaps three or four miles an hour. Just barely rolling to a stop so that no sound would come of the brakes grinding sharply on the crushed stone.

The giant ran in a stooped position and covered the distance of perhaps ten feet that separated him from the car in less than two good strides. Even hunched way over his great curved back stood higher than the top of the car. He ducked low. They could only see him as a fleeting figure, a moving shadow. The car seemed to lurch sidewise, tipped up and was hurled over on its side with a bang as the gigantic figure came up. There came the sound of crashing glass. For the moment King and Luga were both too astonished to move. The great figure could only be seen indistinctly and was going at lightning speed. He bent over and then heaved upward bringing one screaming figure in each hand from the broken windows of the car. The giant seemed to be holding two men up as if they were rag dolls. Silence. Then the two shadowy figures moved apart and came together with terrific force. There was the sound of bone crashing against bone.

Tac! Tac! Tac!

THERE WAS the stutter of a Thompson machinegun echoing in the night air. Bullets whined through the trees. One screamed as it ricocheted off a tree at an angle and soared into the night. But as the gun sounded, the giant bent down once more and two other figures came out of the car. He held them as he had held the others. Tore them literally from the car window. Held and hurled them together to crush skull against skull.

"Come on," King hissed. "Let's go."

He dashed out of the thicket with Luga close behind him. Ran straight for the shadow of the giant of a man. The monster hesitated and turned as though he were coming toward them. Then he seemed to stop and think a moment. The other members of the Secret 6 were tearing on from all sides. King could see their figures dimly in what little light there was on the lawn of the estate. The giant was still hunched over from slamming the last of the bodies down on top of the overturned car. He whirled around and started on a dead run in great strides across the lawn of the estate. King snapped on his flash light—snapped it on just in time to see the great figure leap high into the air and vault the hedge. Then he and the other members of the Secret 6 were after him like a pack of hounds. The hedge was too high for them to leap over. They could hear the sounds of the crashing feet as they pounded the earth and tore the shrubbery of the adjoining estate. The giant was running like a wild man and was getting away so quickly that they couldn't even follow his great form. They could only follow the sound his feet made as they grew dimmer and dimmer.

King stopped breathless.

"Wait," he panted, "I've got another idea. If we stop chasing this giant he'll slow up too. Let's go back to Pennington and find out just what has happened. I got a little hunch and I'd like to find out whether it's true or not."

They retraced their steps and broke through the hedge. They reached the middle of the front lawn and stopped again. King glanced at the flower bed straight ahead of him and to the others at his right. And then to the dim circle with the hideous bodies draped over the car.

"Say," he said hurriedly, "I just thought of something. You men can set the car right side up again and stuff the bodies inside. Somebody has probably called up the police somewhere around this neighborhood. Then after you get the bodies in there be mighty careful of leaving any finger prints where they can be seen and push the car out and down the road two or three estates. Just let it run into the ditch and leave it there for some-

The giant was holding two men as if they were rag dolls.

one else to find. Then come back. I've got a little investigation of my own to do here. I have a hunch. And say, Bishop, maybe, it will be just as well if you said a prayer or so over those dead bodies to ease all of our consciences."

"Of course," agreed the Bishop, "doubtless they don't deserve it but probably it is our duty."

While the other members of the band went on to do as King had suggested, King himself walked to the garden that Pennington had told him the footprints were in. He stared down in the light of his electrical torch and found one of the footprints. There was no denying the size of that one. It was the print of a giant shoe. The heel and the instep and the sole were plainly visible in the soft earth of the flower bed even though they had been made the night before. He found another one and then another across the flower bed. He examined each separately. One queer thing he saw about it was that the toe was uniformly round—round and wide, and there was no difference in the curve on either the left or right like there is in the shape of a normal foot.

Then he found other lighter footprints beside those of the giant. Footprints of a normal sized shoe. Suddenly he straightened and smiled.

"It looks very much," he said, "as though the giant joined those thugs at their own game."

He took a collapsible rule from his pocket and measured the footprints. The print of the shoe measured twenty-three and one-half inches in length. He whistled. "Phew! That's a big foot," he said. "I wonder if it was really a shoe that made that print."

Then he heard the pounding of running feet coming toward

him. He looked up. It was the Key. He held a strange looking instrument in his hand.

"Look what we found in the car," Key said, "I think this is the shoe you're looking for."

King took it and stared at it. It was a make-shift wooden contraption. It was made of a board eight inches wide and about two feet long. One end was rounded off and then about the center it curved in a little like the instep of a shoe. The other end was rounded off too, but it was narrow and on that narrow end was a wide block of wood that would make the mark of a heel. The top had a handle nailed on for carrying it. King took it and with the light of his flashlight fitted it to the footprint in the soft earth of the garden. It fitted perfectly. He grinned up at the Key.

"Where did you find this?" he asked, "in the car?"

"Yeah," said the Key, "I guess they carried it under the back seat and when the giant tipped the car up it fell out from behind the cushion, and while we're talking about the car come on over and see who we got. That is I think we're right. Their heads are pretty mashed in to tell for sure."

King rose and followed him. He stared at the figures as they sat slumped in the seat of the car where the other members of the Secret 6 had placed them. It was a pretty gory spectacle but he managed to make out enough of the faces of three of them to know they were Mark Fiddler, Tony and Al his two henchmen, and one other whom they had never seen.

"All dead?" he asked.

"I'll say they're dead," the Key grinned. "And they're probably handing over their credentials at the gates of hell right now. Boy when the Bishop finishes saying prayers over guys like these—"

"O.K.," said King, "let's get this car out of here and down the road about two or three estates so that they will not be asking Mr. Pennington about the noise."

They pushed the car out of the drive and down the road a good quarter of a mile or more, set it in motion, headed it for a tree down the hill and let it go. There came a terrific crash as the car collided with the tree, folded up, and went over on its side.

"I think," King said, "that's an accident that Fiddler and his two boys won't get out of. Now let's go back. I want to have a little talk with Mr. Pennington and put him at ease and then we will start out after the giant. Do you think you can trail him Luga?"

"Yes, master," replied the black.

"Alright. I'll be with you in just a few minutes. I'll meet you back there the other side of the estate where we left the giant's trail. We'll track him from there."

KING RETRACED his steps towards the house. As he walked toward the drive he kicked the stones about so that in the morning light the blood stains on them wouldn't show so much. He walked up and rang the front door bell. The door was opened instantly this time.

"Good heavens, man, what's happened?" Mr. Pennington demanded hoarsely. "I didn't dare go out but I have been on pins and needles waiting to hear reports. I heard such sounds out there and I think it sounded like machine guns."

King closed the door and slipped in.

"Yes," he said, "it was a machine gun alright but the man that fired that gun and the rest of the men with him in the car won't do any damage to you or anyone else from now on."

"You mean they're dead," he asked.

"Very dead indeed."

They entered the room where they had been before in the light. The rest of the house was still dark.

"I'll tell you as much about it as I can," King said, "because I'm afraid after this racket that the police will come in."

"Good Heavens," Pennington said, "I can't afford to explain all this to the police."

"You won't have to, I don't believe," King said. "If you'll do as I tell you."

He told what had happened.

"Isn't it strange," he said, "that the giant should come and save you from these other men?"

"It's ghastly," said Pennington.

"Well, call it what you like," King said, "but it looks very much to me as though this giant had been in on the deal. I rather imagine he is a henchman of Mark Fiddler whom he killed. Somehow he had an idea that Fiddler was going to pull this deal without him and he came out here to get even with him—and certainly did."

"But what about the tracks in the garden made last night," Pennington asked.

"We have a wooden shoe-form that made those marks," said King. "Those marks were made purposely to carry out the signature of the giant on the end of the message but the giant didn't have anything to do with it last night. But he certainly was here tonight. However, I think Mr. Pennington your worries are over so far as this blackmailing deal is concerned. I'd destroy that note entirely.

"Here is one thing you might do though. Out there by the entrance of the drive just inside the main road there's a considerable amount of blood which might not look so good if the police came to investigate things. Perhaps you'd better get up just a little before dawn tomorrow morning because your lawn needs sprinkling out there by that end of the drive. And don't forget it. It won't hurt the stones a bit if you sprinkle them thoroughly with water until the blood has gone completely out of sight."

"Thank you very much," said Pennington, "that's a very good idea. And rest assured," he almost smiled, "that the lawn will be sprinkled tomorrow morning, where it will do the most good. As a matter of fact, I'll stay up all night so that I'll be up in time to do it."

Suddenly a sound came to King from outside. It was the screaming whine of a police siren.

"Quick," he said, "somebody has called the police. Now listen to me. I'm going to try to keep you out of this. I haven't got time to tell you what to say. Run to your room and take off your coat and shoes. Put on your dressing gown and slippers. Have you got a dim light in the hall?"

"Yes," said Pennington a little breathless, "we have one of those hi-low affairs that you can turn dim or bright. We use the dim on all night sometimes."

"Good just show me where to turn on the dim one and I'll

take care of everything. There's a bus that runs down past this house?"

"Yes," said Pennington.

"O.K., we're all set now. Get going. Your smoking jacket and your slippers, remember."

The police siren was screaming outside on the highway. They were out on the hill right in front of the house from the cry of the siren.

"I only hope they don't see the blood out there in the light of the car," King said as he waited, "if they do we'll have to cook up another story. Remember, let me do the talking."

Pennington hurried into another room on the main floor of the house. Then there were footsteps running on the porch. Police pounded on the door and rang the bell. They couldn't see anything through the windows because the light was out inside. Mr. Pennington came out a moment later with slippers and a smoking jacket on. He hurried into the den and closed the door behind him. King straightened his clothing to put up a neat appearance. More pounding on the front door and ringing the doorbell. "Open up. What's happened?" Some heavy fist seemed about to batter the door in.

"Just a moment," King said, "until I find the light." He found it and switched it on. He took a long breath and stepped to the door. If they recognized him he'd have to think very fast. Perhaps they wouldn't if he kept his face in the shadow of that dim light.

Several voices cried at once:

"What's been going on here?"

"Just be patient," King answered, "until I get the door

unlocked. There you are now." He swung the door open. Four members of the state police rushed into the front hall. They stared at him with keen eyes that were none too pleasant to meet when you know you are in a tight spot.

"Who are you?" demanded one of them.

"I'm Mr. Pennington's chauffeur," King said in as level a voice as he could.

"Huh," sang out one of the police. He came over and looked closely at him: "Don't try to kid me. You're not Penningtons' chauffeur. I've seen him in the big car of Pennington's many a time. You're not him—who are you?"

CHAPTER 10
PATH OF SLAUGHTER

KING FELT like leaping past these troopers piling through the open door but he knew he wouldn't get very far that way. His better judgment told him to be very calm and cool. He bowed more to keep his face in the shadow than to be polite to the troopers.

"Very well," he said, "I hope you'll believe Mr. Pennington himself. I'll see if I can arouse him."

The suspicious trooper walked behind him as he made his way to the den near the rear of the hall. He knocked gently on the door and he said in a low voice: "Mr. Pennington. Please, Mr. Pennington." There came the sound of someone stirring in the den. Then Mr. Pennington opened it with a blank look on his face and blinked at them with well-feigned drowsiness.

"Oh, it's you John," he said. "Did you—" he stopped short and stared at the trooper behind him. Mr. Pennington was acting his part well. "Why, is something wrong. I must have dozed. I was reading and—"

"Pardon me," said King, "these troopers just came bursting into your house. I don't know any more than the fact they asked me who I was and I told them I was your chauffeur and this—er—gentleman here says I'm a liar. He says he knows your chauffeur."

Pennington stared at the trooper. "Oh, yes," he said, "of course—you know Ben. John here is my new chauffeur. He has been in my employ only a short time."

The trooper looked rather sheepish. "Alright, Mr. Pennington," he said, "but we have to make sure, you know."

"Of course, of course," Mr. Pennington said, coming out into the hall and walking toward the front door. "And now that you have that checked up—" He waited.

"We got called up here," the same trooper said, "by somebody in the neighborhood who thought they heard shooting over towards this house a few minutes ago. They called up trooper headquarters and we came right over. They said it sounded like a machine gun going off, and they heard some yelling too."

Mr. Pennington looked blankly from the trooper to King and back.

"Well really," he said, "I can't say as to that. You see I've been asleep in the library. Did you hear anything, John?"

King nodded, still managing to keep his face up out of the light.

"I was just about to waken you about it, Mr. Pennington," he said, "when the troopers came rushing up and rang the doorbell. As you know, Mr. Pennington, I have been out for the evening. I was just coming back on the bus and as I was walking up from the stop down the road I heard quite a lot of excitement. It seemed to come from well down ahead of me."

"You mean it wasn't near this place," Pennington corrected.

"No," King said, "it was, I'd say much farther down the road. In fact, I was right in front of your place the other side of the hedge when I first heard it. That was quite a few minutes ago. I heard someone yelling as though he were being murdered. Then it sounded like a machine gun going off. It was very rapid fire. When I heard the men yelling I started down to see what the excitement was but when I heard the machine gun jabbering down there I changed my mind. So I came back here and came in the back way as usual. I was just coming through the house wondering if I should awaken you or call the police about it when the troopers came up the drive. That's really all I can tell you about it."

The troopers turned and started for the door. "Which way was that you said?" another one demanded.

King went to the door with him and pointed. He pointed in the direction of the trees several estates away where they had crashed the car.

"Down that way," he said, "I heard some glass break too or thought I did. You may find the glass if you can't find anything else."

"O.K.," said the trooper. The four of them started out of the door again and walked swiftly to their car and climbed in. They backed out of the drive with a rush and tore down the road. King came in and shut the door. He smiled at Mr. Pennington as he took a long breath.

"Well," he said, "I think that takes care of that matter all right."

"Phew!" whistled Pennington, "that was close."

"It was close enough for me too," said King, "but now I think the best thing you can do is to turn in, Mr. Pennington. And I'll be on my way. I don't believe the troopers will bother you again tonight or at all in fact. If they should want me again you might just tell them that after they left I went out. You thought I went to see how they were coming on with the investigation. There will probably be a crowd down there and I could very well be lost in it if I were there—and of course I won't be."

Pennington held out his hand. "Young man," he sighed, "I'm eternally grateful for what you have done. I was about to go crazy when you first came in. You know a man dreads to think of a thing like this particularly after he has made good in his later years. I've always tried to make my money with fair dealing and it was dreadful to suddenly realize that there were men who could ruin me, particularly when they could do it without just cause. Well the thing is simply maddening that's all."

"I can understand that," King said. "And with those four dead in the car I don't believe you need have any more worry. Good night, Mr. Pennington."

He turned the light in the hall so that no one could see him silhouetted there. "And don't forget to water the lawn and driveway thoroughly, Mr. Pennington," he grinned.

"Indeed I won't," said Pennington as he closed the door.

KING HURRIED toward the place where he was to meet the other members of the Secret 6. He pushed through the hedge noiselessly. He could see lights of cars shinning against the trees farther down the road where the car had crashed. He smiled to himself as he went on.

He reached the spot where the others were waiting for him.

"How did you make out then," the Key asked.

"Yes, we were all wondering," said the Bishop. "We felt that perhaps we'd have to come back and rescue you from the police."

"Somebody in the neighborhood must have 'phoned," King said, "when they heard the yelling and shooting. I certainly thought that they had me for a minute there. You see I told Mr. Pennington to go in the den and pretend he had fallen asleep after reading. Then I answered the door and told them that I was his chauffeur. The only trouble was that one trooper knew his chauffeur. We almost went round and round for a minute until I got Mr. Pennington awake so he could verify my statement. They finally believed that I was a new chauffeur just taken on. I told them I heard the sound too and sent them down where they'd find the car crashed into the tree where we had left it." He turned to the dark form just behind him at his right. "Think you can pick up the trail, Luga?"

"Yes, master," Luga said. "Luga already follow it at hedge just beyond there. We go now?"

"Right," said King.

Luga followed that trail with the instinct of a bloodhound. Now and then it was necessary for him to turn on his flash light where the ground grew harder and he couldn't follow it with ease. Then again they moved on through the darkness. The trail led them to the east, back toward the hideout but still miles away from it.

They walked on for two hours following Luga as he trailed the giant. The signs showed that the giant had stopped running and was continuing on his way in great strides. Another hour passed. They came out into a village. Then suddenly they stopped. Not a word of warning had been sounded by any one of the group. They all seemed to see the confusion ahead at the same time. A group of people were huddled about a store in the village.

"Suppose," suggested the Doctor, "that I go down and see what has happened. I'm not apt to be recognized like some of the rest of you."

"Good idea," agreed King. "We'll wait here for you."

The Doctor strode off down the little street. The group waited in the shadow of a building.

"There's certainly something up," King said. "That many people wouldn't congregate in this little town at midnight for anything short of a fire or maybe a murder."

"It seems to be right in the path of the giant as we're trailing him," observed the Bishop. "I wonder if it's something he could have done as he went through the town?"

"I can't figure anything else," said King. "We'll know all about it in a minute. There comes the Doctor. He's coming back now."

The Doctor reached them shaking his head.

"What a man that giant must be!" he said. "It all seemed to happen about half or three-quarters of an hour ago as near as I can learn. Everybody is congregated out there in front of that butcher shop. The front door is smashed right in and a good part of the plate glass front went in with it. The place looks as if a rhinoceros has hit it. The butcher is wild. He heard the excitement and came down in time to see a giant figure running up the street. He says he's lost two or three hundred pounds of hams and beef."

"Phew," whistled King, "apparently when the giant gets hungry he doesn't fool around kidding his appetite any. Let's go. We'd better take a back street until we circle the crowd and butcher shop then we can come back and hit the trail again."

Then he stopped for a moment.

"Say!" he ejaculated. "We're right on the main highway now. If someone goes back and gets the sedan from here and drives it along after us it will save us walking so far to get back to it. We might have good use for it."

"Suppose," the Doctor suggested, "I go back."

"Fine," said King, "you might be able to catch a bus as far as you want to go and that would save you walking. That's if there are buses running this time of the night."

The Doctor left them to go back. The others skirted the group in the street by going round the block. Then they came back to the main highway again and walked on. Here the hard surface road made it difficult to identify the marks left by the giant. The only thing they could do was to take it for granted that the giant had passed that way.

"Let's split up," King said. "Luga, you and the Bishop will take the left, and Shakespeare, the Key and I will take the right hand side of the road."

They moved on in that way. Now and then cars coming caused them to take to the side of the road and duck out of sight until they had passed. Then they resumed their trailing and several times found marks in the earth and in the bushes at the side of the road where the giant had likewise to let a car pass. Once in the light of his torch King found a good clear print of a giant foot in the soft soil on the left hand side of the road. Instantly he stooped, took out a collapsible rule and measured it. He whistled softly.

"Man, oh—man!" he said. "What a foot that giant has. I thought that was a big wooden shoe mark that was in the garden at Pennington's place that measured 23½ inches but this foot is too big for any shoe. See it's the print of bare foot—a perfectly normal human foot, and it measures thirty-one inches. Imagine that for a foot! Almost a yard long. Why this fellow must be the biggest man in the world. I've never heard of anything like it."

THEY STRODE on for another hour and not once did they find the track of the giant moved from the road. In fact they saw no more footprints. They heard a car coming slowly down the road from the east. The lights were blinking off and on.

"The rest of you duck," King said, "it's probably the Doctor scaring us but we can't take any chances with the whole crowd. I'll stand out and hail it and you stay away out of sight. If I need any help you can come in from the rear."

The others hid in the brush in that side of the road while

King stood out boldly on the road and hailed the car. The lights blinked faster at him. Then the car slowed and stopped beside him. The Doctor's face peered out of the window at him.

"Any dope yet?" he asked.

"Not at all," King answered. "I'm afraid we've lost the trail now that we are on the road."

The others came from the side and gathered about the car.

"Personally," drawled Shakespeare, "I could do with a little riding myself."

"I think that would be a good idea for all of us," King said. "There's a dirt road back here about a quarter of a mile. Suppose we all climb in the car and pull back there and try to get a wink of sleep. Either the giant has stuck completely to the road or we've missed the place where he has turned off in the darkness. A man as big as that isn't apt to turn back and head for the city if he knows all the police in seven counties are after him."

They climbed in the car. King turned to the Doctor.

"Did you ever hear of a man," he asked, "with a bare foot that was 31 inches long?"

"Great Scott! What are you talking about?" the Doctor demanded.

"Just that," retorted King, "we found one of his footprints in the soft earth beside the road about an hour ago and it measured 31 inches by my rule."

"I never heard of such a thing," said the Doctor.

"Nor I," added the Bishop.

"Nor I," Shakespeare concurred.

"Stop and think what that means," said the Doctor. "The average man six feet tall wears a shoe somewhere between 12 and 15 inches long. Fifteen inches, that is, if he has particularly large feet. I've heard of one or two mammoth southern men who had feet almost twenty-four inches long but they were nearly seven feet tall and had abnormally large feet. But a bare foot 31 inches long! That's beyond my powers of comprehension. Why a man with feet that size unless he were a circus freak would have to be nine or ten or even eleven feet tall."

"That's what I've been thinking," said King as the car turned around and they started back to the side road. There they turned in and pulled off in a flat space at the side of the road. They were well crowded with three in each seat but they managed to slump down until their heads rested on the back of the seat. They closed their eyes.

Shakespeare was the first to start snoring. Then the Bishop cut in with some very healthy competition of his own. Others showed signs of falling asleep. King was almost dropping off when he heard a rear door of the car open softly. He turned his head quickly. The big black form of Luga loomed in the rear tonneau.

"Where you going, Luga?" he whispered.

The big black whispered back. "Luga get out. Make more room. Luga lay down on ground beside car."

"Not a bad idea," King thought. He reached behind him and took the car robe and opened the door softly on his side and stepped out.

"I think I'll do the same," he whispered. He stretched out on the ground rolled up in the blanket. Closed his eyes and presently fell asleep.

KING WOKE up with a start. Luga was bending over him shaking him gently. The sun was just breaking over the horizon.

"Master, come. Time to get up. Luga find trail."

King got up instantly.

"Good boy," he said, "where did we lose it?"

"Luga find trail turn off just where car come and pick us up," the big black said.

"Nice work," said King.

He got up and shook out the blanket and folded it. Opened the rear door of the car and slid it in the robe rack.

"Come on you birds," he called to the four sleeping inside, "breakfast isn't ready but it's time to get up."

The men awoke sleepily rubbing their eyes.

"Good Heavens," said the Doctor, "I never would have believed I could actually sleep with a giant floating around loose and only a front seat behind the wheel for a bed."

"I find it easy to sleep in any position," said Shakespeare, "when I'm tired."

"You were sure sleeping, alright," shrugged the Key, "from the sound of that saw mill you were dreaming about. Boy when you go in for actions you don't mess with them do you?"

They piled out of the car one by one and stood on the ground stretching and yawning.

"And now what?" said the Doctor.

"We're going after the giant again," King said. "Luga found

the trail. It left the road just a little beyond where you picked us up. Which way did he turn off, Luga?"

"He turn off to right," Luga said.

"Oh he's headed south," said King, "into the interior of Long Island. Say that's a fairly wild country down there too. Apparently he seems to know where he is going."

"Apparently," said the Doctor caustically, "he knows entirely too much for a man his size."

"Do we—er—ride after him in the car?" Shakespeare asked.

"No," said Luga, "we walk. He left road and went across the fields. We cannot go by car."

King ventured. "We might just as well leave the car here if we can't take it with us. This is good a place to park as any."

They struck off toward the main highway and turned right. Walked perhaps one-quarter of a mile beyond the point where the Doctor had picked them up in the darkness. Luga was ahead leading the way.

"Here," he said, "see where the big foot stamped down grass."

An exclamation left the Doctor's lips as he saw the tracks that showed where a great weight had pressed down the brown autumn grass. They followed silently after that. Luga leading the way. The trail was very easy to follow, leading straight across country through little valleys and up hills. Fair sized bushes were crushed down where the foot of the giant had tread on them in the darkness. The giant had walked in great strides. There was almost six feet of space between each print of his feet.

"How that guy can cover ground," the Key marveled.

"And that's not all he can do," King observed. "That fellow

has got all the strength he needs, I imagine. A man big enough to take hold of the running board of a low hanging car like that sedan and tip it up on its side with four men in it, is some man!" He paused.

"What I'd like to know," King said, "is whether that was Mark Fiddler and some of his men in that sedan that chased us yesterday afternoon and just what happened to them?"

"It was the same car," the Key said. "I looked it over pretty thoroughly last night when we tipped it back and stuck the guys back in. The one side of the car that was up showed plainly the marks of a crash.

"The fenders were quite badly crumpled up on that side too. They probably got a tow car from some garage to pull them up and had the damage fixed up in time to come out to Penny-feathers or whatever the guy's name is."

"Pennington," corrected the Bishop. "We're coping with a master man physically if not mentally."

"Yeah," said the Key, "well don't kid yourself. This giant guy is no feather weight in his bean either. He knows what he is doing."

They had come over a little rise of ground and now were dropping down into what seemed to be an old quarry. The tracks lead down that way.

"What's this?" King asked. "It looks like an abandoned mine."

"Jolly," said the Bishop, "I wonder if this isn't the old gypsum mine that I've heard was out here somewhere on Long Island. It's been abandoned for years. Seems to me I read a newspaper story a year ago called 'The Prospector of Long Island' or something like that. It had to do with an old prospector who was a little off in his mind prospecting this old gypsum mine for gold, or something of that kind."

"Looks to me," observed the King, "as though the Giant knew all about it. His tracks lead right down into the mine."

As they came closer they saw a one-room shack, old and tumbled-down in one corner of the pit. And across from it toward the side of the hill over which they had just come was a hole in the ground that led straight back into the hill. There was a pile of debris out in front of it that had apparently just been thrown out.

King stared about the place, and then suddenly he stopped short, his eyes focused on something near the end of the cabin. A cry escaped his lips and he pointed.

"Look!" he said.

CHAPTER 11
BLOOD OGRE

FOR THAT instant every member of the Secret 6 stood stock still and stared in the direction King's finger was pointing. Then suddenly King rushed forward and the others were beside him as he bent over a still limp broken form lying just at the edge of some bushes in the end of the shack. The figure was laying face upward on the ground. Its white flowing beard was smeared with blood. The face and head were mashed almost beyond recognition.

"Golly," cried the Bishop in an awestricken voice, "that must be the old prospector that I read about. The one that the papers had such a laugh with. He has been murdered."

"Murdered hel—goodness, I mean," exploded the Key. "It looks more like he has been run over with a steam roller."

King stared about the ground near the body. The ground was hard enough to make a clear foot print almost impossible still they could see the pressure of the great feet of the giant where he had trodden the earth. Part of the side of the shack was broken in. The Doctor pointed to it. To a mark that was covered with blood on one of the boards.

"Look there," he said, "the giant must have picked up the poor old man as he came out of his shack last night and hurled him like a cannon ball against the side of the building. There is one thing I'm sure enough of now. Last night we kept from shooting this giant because we weren't sure whether he deserved killing or not. If we get a crack at him we'll not stop for anything. We'll kill him the first chance we get and there'll not be a question asked."

"I thought last night when he killed Mark Fiddler and his three men that there might be some excuse because Fiddler and his men deserved to die but this is going too far. There is no reason why an old prospector, or an old man who thinks he's a prospector, should die just because he is a little off in the head. Why, this giant is the worst killer I've ever heard of. The man must be mad," said King.

He walked to the entrance of the shack. He peered inside. He had his automatic loose in his hand when he did so but the shack was empty. There was a small wood stove in one corner of the shack, a bunk with dirty old blankets heaped in disorder in the other, and a little stand with a candle in a bottle in the center. Those were the only things that King saw except for a pick and shovel standing next to the door. These obviously were the only tools—or weapons that matter—that the old prospector had owned. King picked them up and held them with his free hand.

"I think," he said, "it would be no more than fitting for the old fellow to get a decent burial. What do you think Bishop?"

"Of course," replied the Bishop, "and I'll be more than glad to officiate in any capacity I can."

"I dig grave, master," Luga said coming forward and taking the shovel and pick from King's hands, "you show me where."

King glanced about.

"I don't think it needs very much," he said, "suppose you dig a hole right about there a few feet from the shack. It won't need to be very deep because we have plenty more to do today."

"Yes master," said Luga. Then he went to work while the dirt flew and the grave got deeper and deeper. King took a blanket from the bunk and he and Shakespeare proceeded to roll the remains of the old prospector in it. Then when the grave was finished and while the Bishop recited the burial sermon they lowered the prospector into the grave. They stood about while Luga filled the hole and patted it down with the shovel. That finished, they turned away. King jerked his head toward the entrance of the mine.

"I think next we'll go in there," he said. "There's no telling what we may find and we can't take chances with this giant from now on."

They moved across the front of the open quarry toward the

hole in the bank and came to a place in the center of it where the earth was soft and smooth and loose. It was the Bishop who exploded then.

"Jolly!" he exclaimed, "look there." He pointed a stubby finger at the ground to the right of them where the soft earth was.

King blinked and stared. There before them were giant foot prints clearly marked in the soft earth. King bent down to examine them without spoiling the footmarks.

"See," the Key yelled, "unless I'm crazy, one of those feet is bigger than the other one. Get out your measure, King, and see how it racks up."

King was already bending down with his collapsible rule extended. He measured the small footprint first.

"This measures 35 inches more or less," he said."

"I don't think we need argue about fractions when we get feet this big."

The Doctor was staring hard as King measured.

"That foot you just measured, King—is it from the right foot?" he queried. "I think the Key is correct. This other foot print sure does look larger. It is the print of a left foot. Suppose you measure that and we'll see how they compare."

King got up and moved over. "Forty-one inches," he declared. He got up and stared blankly at the other members of his band. "Say," he exclaimed, "that's the funniest thing I've heard of yet. We trail that giant all the way from the place where he robbed the meat market—assuming he robbed the meat market later found a footprint on the side of the road measuring 31 inches. And here the small one measures 35."

"Do you remember," the Doctor asked, "whether the footprint at the side of the road that you measured was a right or a left foot."

Key shook his head.

"I'm afraid I don't," he said. "Any of the rest of you remember?"

They all shook their heads in negative.

"What difference would it make?" King asked. "That footprint was 31 inches and this small one was 35 inches and we have another one here that measures 41 inches."

"Only this," said the Doctor, "and it is the only answer I can put forward. Wouldn't it be possible for a man to shorten up his foot print to a certain extent? Suppose a normal person's bare foot measures twelve inches long. Suppose he was to step on something sharp that caught him in the instep, the most tender part of the foot."

"Tender it is," laughed King. "Particularly when you're burned with a cigarette."

"Alright," said the Doctor, "now let's suppose a normal person should step on something sharp that came up in the instep. That would cause an instant contraction of the foot if he walked on the heel and the ball of the foot as most people do. The toes would automatically double up to take the weight of the instep off the sharp thing they had trod on.

"Perhaps whatever it was that hurt the instep would stay in his foot and they would have to lift it up and take it out. That would show you a footprint perhaps a full inch shorter than normal until the cause for it had been removed."

"Do you mean to tell me," King demanded, "that a giant like

this might have one foot of 35 inches and the other six inches longer?"

"It's possible, you know," said the Doctor, "and here's something else that you'll probably realize if you remember buying any shoes at all. As the usual thing the left foot is larger than the right foot. That tallies up perfectly with this situation."

"But six inches larger," King argued, "that's going a little too far, isn't it?"

"Perhaps a little," said the Doctor, "but of course you've got to learn this. We're now dealing with a freak and we can't apply normal conditions to him at any time."

"Alright, that seems to take care of that so far," King said. "Now let's take a look in the mine."

The group broke up and they moved on across the flat of the old quarry toward the hole in the side of the hill. Suddenly King stopped and stared ahead of him. There were more foot prints of a giant bare foot plainly outlined ahead of him.

"There's one thing for you," he said. "Explain that, Doctor, if you can."

AGAIN THE group stopped. Here before them were several prints of bare feet showing plainly in the soft earth, some tangled with others as the giant seemed to hesitate, and here were marks of just the toes and the soles of the foot. Two or three of those and they turned and headed toward the shack.

"I wonder," mused King, "if this wouldn't explain it. The giant came down here in the quarry and looked around until he spotted the opening to the mine that the prospector had probably spent years in digging. The prospector woke up and heard him,

116

went outside of his shack and demanded to know what he was doing. Then the giant turned quickly and ran to the shack and killed the old prospector. In the prints it shows that the giant was apparently running. Look at the length of those strides. They must be almost ten feet long."

"Very likely that was the story," the Doctor said.

"Alright," said Key, "we've got that O.K. but here's something perhaps you haven't noticed."

He bent down and measured one of the prints in the soft dirt. That led to the point where the giant had turned and ran back toward the shack.

"This one," King said, "is 35 inches long like the other one."

"Well what of it," said the Doctor.

"Look a little closer Doctor," said King. "You remember the footprint that we measured before that was 35 inches long was the print of the right foot. This is the print of the left foot."

The Doctor bent down and stared hard.

"By George!" he exploded, "you're right."

"But here's something else," said King. He bent down beside another footprint and measured it. "This one is 41 inches."

The Doctor studied that. "Yes," he said, "but that's the print of a left foot also."

"Right," agreed King, "but let's try this next one." He moved back six or seven feet toward the opening of the mine on the edge of the loose dirt. "Here's a right footprint," he said. "Let's measure the length of this and see how we come out." He squatted beside it ran his measure the length of the footprint. "This one is a right print and it measures 41 inches."

117

"Jolly!" said the Bishop, "what do you make of that?"

"Simply this," said King, getting up and taking a long breath. "It looks to me like we're up against a much bigger proposition than we ever dreamed of. We have the print of a right and a left foot here that measures 35 inches and we also have the print of a right and a left foot that measures 41 inches. If it means anything at all it means that we're dealing with two giants instead of one."

"That's exactly it," said the Doctor. "We've been all wrong or at least I have in guessing that one foot was larger than the other. Two giants were here last night in the quarry instead of one. They met here."

"Yes," said King, "and the queer part of the whole thing is this most astonishing part. In fact, it seems that the giant that we saw last night or—his shadow—was the biggest human thing we ever saw in our life. If he is human and still as big as he was, he was the smaller of these two who met here last night."

Everyone fell silent for a moment. Then slowly King turned to the Doctor.

"Doctor," he requested, "take a good look at those prints. Is there anything about them that would make you believe that they're the foot prints of a giant ape or gorilla?"

After a close examination, the Doctor shook his head.

"No," he said, "those look like perfectly normal human feet of huge size. In the foot of a gorilla for instance, the toes are much longer than human toes, and they're shaped differently."

The Doctor turned to Luga.

"Now you have seen plenty of gorillas in your country in Africa, haven't you, Luga?" he asked.

The black man nodded.

"Yes," he said, "many times."

"The print of a gorilla," the Doctor went on, "of the gorilla foot I mean is more like the print of a hand, isn't it?"

"Yes," said Luga, "gorilla foot like hand. Fingers and thumb are longer than on human foot."

"But listen," King said, "isn't the gorilla foot much longer for its size than the foot of a human being?"

"Yes, master," said Luga, "much bigger."

"Have you ever seen the track of a gorilla as long as this?"

"No, master," said Luga, "biggest gorilla track I ever see maybe about half as big as this biggest track. Master, this no gorilla track Luga know. Gorilla track like print of a hand more."

King took a deep breath.

"I guess that settles that," he said. "Apparently we're trailing two giant men and we can't in the wildest stretches of our imagination figure them out as anything else. Now let's go into the mine. Keep your lights and your guns ready and don't hesitate to shoot and shoot to kill if we're attacked. These giants are not anything to play with any more."

KING WENT first into the opening of the mine. Luga followed close behind him and at one side. The entrance was a large affair perhaps ten or twelve feet in height. It seemed to cease to be a mine after they entered fifteen or twenty feet into the depths. It became a cave in the side of the hill. Except for the little light that shone in through the entrance, the vaulted reaches beyond them were dark as pitch. They penetrated the darkness with the beams of their flash lights and moved on and on into the depths. Moved with great caution and stealth.

The corners might easily hide one of the two giants or both. The giants might leap out suddenly from the dark cavernous depths and envelope all six of them in their arms and crush them before they even had a chance.

Shakespeare stopped and called softly. King hesitated and turned back.

"What is it, Shakespeare?" he asked in a tense voice.

"I've just been considering something," Shakespeare said. "I trust you won't think me timid, but suppose these two giants or even one of them are in this mine here. Either of them will be large enough for our bullets will make little impression. That will mean that if we don't hit them in a vital spot the first time they may come on and kill us all before we have any chance to kill them."

"I've thought of that too," said King, "but I don't know exactly what we're going to do about it."

"We might," the Doctor suggested, "smoke them out. Like you'd smoke foxes out of their dens."

"All of that," said King, "would take time. Have you any idea how far back this mine goes? Perhaps it would be best if I lay out the plan as I have it in mind and we'll all see what we can do about it. To me the most important thing is that we get these giants and kill them. That sounds like quite a proposition I know but it is the only way we're going to stop this infernal murder and blackmail. The giants apparently have control of those records that were stolen from the D.A.'s office."

"I have been wondering," said the Key, "how you tie up the giant who beat up Mark Fiddler with the man who took the records. You said Flo told you that he was probably about seven feet tall. Why, he is a little puny guy compared with these big fellows unless they've got awful big feet."

"It might be," King said, "that he's the one with the 35 inch foot. Although it would sound awful large to me for a man seven feet tall to have feet 35 inches long. And to tell you the truth if this man that Flo saw had feet that were almost a yard long I think perhaps she would have noticed it and said something about it."

"Oh these dames," mocked the Key, "they wouldn't notice a guy's foot—they're always looking at a guy's face to see how good looking he is."

King smiled.

"I think," he said, "that Flo would take in everything. Faces don't mean an awful lot to her when she can have her pick from a certain class."

"Then you think," the Doctor ventured, "that there may be three giants instead of two?"

King thought that over for a minute.

"Yes," he said, "or perhaps four. If you can call that fellow that was six feet two or-three that Kelly saw coming out of the Mann residence a giant."

"Phew!" whistled the Key, "what a swell set-up for a black-mail racket that is. They can send this guy around that is six feet two or-three and he won't be noticed so much and then if he don't collect from the rich birds the old granddaddy giant can go down and scare the living day-lights out of them, and if they don't come around then he can tear them limb from limb and from then on there wouldn't be any argument from the other rich guys."

"Exactly," said King, "if there's an organization like that going there is no end to what they could do in the blackmail or any other racket. It's the worst menace this country has ever heard of, I'll gamble. People will be afraid to step out of their house at night all over this corner of the United States."

He stared off again deep in thought and started off into the mine.

"Come on," he said, "we've got to finish this up and if they are not in here in this nest of caves we've got to get over and trail them. Men as big as these two can't hide very easily. I'll take a bet on that."

He moved on with the others following. At each step King flashed his light ahead of him and on all sides to make sure that some giant wasn't about to grab him in their great hands. The interior of that cave became a place filled with ominous dread. There was something weird about the whole thing. The suspense was telling on them. King did his best to keep to the main passage. The going was getting rougher now. He climbed over rocks and through narrow passages. The light from outside the entrance was entirely cut off now. They could only see by the glow of the electric torches.

King stopped suddenly. "Wait a minute," he said. "We've each got a flash light. Let's use just two of them at once. There's no telling how long we'll be in this place and we don't want to be left without any lights at all. Two lights on at one time will be plenty. If we can see ahead we're all right."

His voice echoed hollowly through the great cavernous depths. Then another voice echoed in return from the rear.

"Just a minute," the voice boomed hollowly, "it might be possible for one of these giants to come around behind us and cut us off. Hadn't we better watch the rear?"

Instantly every man turned and stared into the darkness behind him.

King felt a chilly sensation around his spine. It was all right to fight when you knew where the enemy was but in this dark spot it was tough on the nerves. The Doctor was probably right in concluding that the cave was a labyrinth of passages, and it would be possible for these giants to come up behind them and cut off any escape.

Then suddenly a sound came that chilled the blood in every man in that cave. It was a slight rustling sound. It came— stopped again.

"What was that?" King hissed. Already the men had bunched together. Flash lights probed the interior down the sharp stone corridors they had just passed. But they saw nothing. The sound stopped instantly.

"I don't know," the Doctor whispered hoarsely, "it came from behind me somewhere near the entrance of the cave."

The sound came again. The men stood motionless. Not one of them breathed. Then came a very gentle thud from where the light shone. Every man of the group gave a start. Every man, that is, except King. He stood waiting, his hand tight on his gun.

CHAPTER 12
THE POINTING FLAME

THE INTERIOR of the cavern became as still as death. There seemed nothing to do but wait. Every second that rolled by seemed like an eternity.

They were waiting for the next sound to come to their ears. They stood for perhaps a full minute like that. Cold sweat poured out on their foreheads. The dread and horror of the whole situation, mingled with the chilly air inside the hole which was part mine, part natural cavern, combined to make them feel clammy all over.

Suddenly King moved.

"There's no sense in standing here any longer," he growled. "I'm going back to find out what that noise was."

He stopped stock still again, for the noise came once more from the same quarter. There was no thud this time as there had been before, but it was that rustling sound that they couldn't make out.

"Alright," he said. "There it is again. Now we're going to find out what it is."

With the light piercing the darkness ahead of him he pushed back past the others. They turned and followed him. Luga, as always, was right beside him or a step behind, as the passage necessitated. He strode perhaps fifty feet back the way they had come, reached a point where one lateral passage came in from the right and another came in from the left slightly beyond that. He shot his light down both passages. He could only see a little way in them for they twisted.

They heard the same rustling sound again for a minute, and then it stopped. Something touched his arm. As he whirled he felt a pressure. It was Luga's hand.

"Master!" he hissed. "Same noise behind."

Again every man tensed to listen. Yes, that rustling sound was coming from the other side.

"I can't figure it out," King said softly. "Sometimes it sounds like someone in skirts slipping up on us, and then when we come back it sounded as if he or she were running away again."

He turned back now the way they had been going when they first came in.

"We might as well go on," he said, loud enough so the others could hear him.

All the lights were on now. King noticed this.

"Remember what I said about only two lights on. Maybe it'll be enough if I just have mine on in the front. And Doctor, you keep yours on in the rear so that we won't be caught in a surprise attack."

"Surely," agreed the Doctor.

All except his and the Doctor's flashlight were off. Now and then they came to places where winding corridors branched off in various directions, some of them back and some of them forward. The place seemed honeycombed with passages leading in every direction.

For perhaps fifteen or twenty minutes they plodded on, climbing over rocks, slipping on the moist treacherous stones. Once they skirted what seemed a black bottomless well. All of that added to the tenseness of the situation. A loose rock shot from under King's foot and hurled into the black pit. Then after a space of what seemed hours they heard the stone strike far, far below.

"Holy Gee," the Key hissed. "What a swell dump for a murder this would be!"

No one answered him.

King moved farther away from the edge of the pit and closer to the wall on his right.

"Keep close behind me," he commanded. "It's a swell place to fall if you aren't careful."

They all managed to get around that bend and moved on. Now the sense of another kind of danger was coming more strongly to King and it helped in some way to counteract the feeling that one of those giants might leap out from the inky shadows. It was the danger of their getting lost in the bowels of the earth. During the next few minutes he did some serious thinking. He studied the vaulted ceilings of the place, stared about them in wonder. He had no idea when they entered the place that it would end in these great fathomless caverns.

Besides that he was getting hungry and he knew the others were too. And a drink of water would taste good. But except for the moisture on the side of the rocky walls there was no water in the place. And there certainly was no food to be had. Then finally he stopped where the passage widened out into a small flat-floored room lined with giant stones.

"I wonder," he said, "if we aren't pretty crazy going on like this. I had an idea when we started that in a very few minutes we could find out whether those giants were in here or not. But from the looks of those caverns and the number of passages in here, a dozen giants could be hiding and we would never find them."

The Bishop spoke up. "It would seem to me," he said, "that a man, even though he was ten or twelve feet tall, could walk standing up straight through these passages and we are constantly coming to lateral passages that lead in almost any direction."

"I wish I knew," King said, "what that sound was that we heard a while ago. If I were sure it wasn't the giant stalking us I would turn around and go back."

"Listen," Luga hissed in his ear. King stood tense to listen.

"There it is again, Master," said Luga. "Nearer."

King's flashlight swung upward and down a corridor to the left. Then suddenly he saw a wildly flapping thing flying through the black air.

At that he laughed, and there was relief in it.

"We should have known," he said. "They're bats. Probably the place is full of them—caves generally are."

"We go back then, Master?" asked Luga.

"I think so," said King. "If that's the only sound we've heard in here I'd be sure enough that the giants weren't in the place.

127

And in that case we might as well get out as quickly as possible and see if we can find out which way they went on the outside."

He started back with Luga at his side and the others trailing. They reached the first group of lateral hallways. King paused.

"I think we came in straight ahead, didn't we, Luga?" he asked.

Luga hesitated. "I think so, Master," he said. "Luga not sure."

King turned the flashlight down to the floor of the cavern and examined it.

"I can't see any footprints at all here," he said.

Luga was looking. Then he shook his head.

"Not show up on rough stones," said the big black. "Luga think we go straight ahead."

King led on. Again and again they came to places where two or three or four other passages led off from around a stalactite that met its stalagmite to form a pillar in the center. Each time King and Luga got down to look at the floor of the cavern to find some footprints there, and each time King did it with a little more desperate zeal for fear of being lost in that maze of caverns. And yet only once did they find a possible mark of a footprint in the hard bottom of the passage.

AN HOUR passed. They were undoubtedly lost. They would have long since passed that bottomless pit that King had kicked the stone into.

They were now treading new territory. They might even be going deeper and deeper into the bowels of the earth for all they knew. They might circle around and around those passages for the rest of their lives.

And the rest of their lives wouldn't be very long without food or water, which there certainly was no chance of getting here. But there was no need of mentioning this to the others. If they didn't know it they would soon enough.

Nerves grew tighter and tighter. The whir and rustling of the bats didn't seem to mean anything to them. As a matter of fact it was the only companionable thing that they could hear aside from their own footsteps.

King tried to joke with himself. Tried to tell himself laughingly, without uttering any audible words, that they might catch bats and eat them. Some of them they had seen recently were big enough. But then that thought didn't hit so well on an empty stomach and he gave up the futile attempt at humor. Now and then he glanced at his wristwatch. They'd been in there entirely too long. It seemed that he glanced at it for the hundredth time when the Key spoke.

"Hey, you mugs! What do you say we get out of here and find a one-armed joint where we can get some grub?"

"Just keep your shirt on for a while."

"Yeah! I know," bawled the Key, "but we've looked all over this place for the giants that aren't in here."

"Be still!" said the Bishop softly. "King's having hard enough time to get us out of here without listening to any complaints."

King stopped now.

"I hope none of you," he said, "think that I've been trying to bluff about knowing my way around. The truth of the matter is we're lost in the maze of endless hallways. I haven't said anything about it before because there was no use of frightening anybody, but I guess you all have the idea by now. I didn't think we were going to get into passageways like this when we came in. My idea in coming here was to trap the giants and kill them. But I'm frank to admit that I'm lost, and if any of you men have the slightest idea as to how we can find our way out I will be grateful."

"Isn't it usually the custom," the Doctor asked, "when going into a cave of this sort to carry along a ball of twine and unroll it as you go so that you can follow it out again?"

"I guess so," King said, "But not having had a ball of twine in the first place, and in the second place not knowing that we were going to get into this—"

"We're stuck, in the third place," the Key added with a chuckle.

"Do any of you know anything about caves?" King asked.

"If we didn't before we came in here," Shakespeare said, "we surely should know something about it now."

"We ought to know enough to keep out of them next time," the Key said. "Especially around meal time."

"Look here," said King. "Isn't there apt to be a circulation of air through a cavern sometimes? Seems to me I felt a breeze on my face at times. A very slight one."

"Yes," said the Doctor, "I believe it depends on the cave. If there are two outlets to it you're very apt to get a draft blowing through. But if there's only the entrance then the air is apt to be pretty dead and damp, and musty and stale."

"How does this smell to you in here, Doctor?" King asked.

"Seems pretty fresh," said the Doctor. "By George, I believe you've hit on something."

"If there's a draft, then," remarked King, "it ought to show up when I light a match, shouldn't it?"

"All right I'll light a match. I'll hold it up where the breeze can get it. We'll see which way it goes."

He struck a match and held it up. The flame blew slightly back the way they had just come.

"There seems to be a draft all right," the Doctor observed. "It's blowing from ahead of us."

"What would you say was the right direction for us to take first?" asked King.

The Doctor shook his head.

"That's a hard matter to determine," he said. "Not having the slightest idea of what the other opening to the cave might be, the chances are that the draft will blow from the lower opening toward the higher opening as what little heat that comes into the cave would rise."

"Just at a guess, then," King said, "I'd say that we ought to go the way that the draft comes from because we entered the cave on the side of a hill. As a matter of fact we entered on the side of the quarry, there. Come on. Let's go."

He led the way once more. Led the way against the draft that blew through the caverns.

King lighted another match. The draft blew at them from two of the passages. King wagged his finger back and forth at the two.

"My mother told me to take this one. This is the one we take."

"I imagine," the Doctor said, "that you'll find both those passages join farther on."

"Likely," said King.

Ten minutes later they came to another series of laterals and again he lighted a match and found that the draft came from straight ahead. They went on that way.

King stopped. Except for the light behind they were plunged in darkness.

"My light has gone," he said. "How about one of yours?"

King took the light from the big black. They moved on, down through that labyrinth of chasms that seemed to stretch endlessly through the depths of the earth.

"Here's my last match," King said at length. "Anybody else got one?"

"I have a few," answered the Doctor.

"I have perhaps a half-dozen," said the Bishop.

"Hey, save some matches," the Key croaked, "I want to have a smoke pretty soon. If I can't eat, maybe I can keep alive for a while by smoking."

"You'll smoke for eternity," King told him, "if we don't get out of here."

Then later Luga's light went out and King took the light of Shakespeare and led on. He used all the matches the Doctor had. The Bishop gave him his half dozen. Then at another point Shakespeare's flashlight grew dim and King flung it away.

"If we ever get back to the cabin," he said, "we're going to get some fresh supplies of flashlights. I can tell you that much."

His nerves were tightening up on him. There was something he didn't like about this underground business. He was too much out of his element. He was a man of the air, not of subterranean passages. The feeling of confinement grew on him, made him feel jittery.

The light that he had gotten from the Bishop went out and he borrowed the one that the Key had. The Doctor had long since turned his flashlight out to save it. They heard the flutter of bat wings above them.

That struck a note of new terror to King. Perhaps they'd taken the wrong direction. He didn't know much about bats, but he knew that they frequented the darkest places they could find. Perhaps they were walking deeper and deeper into the depths of the earth if the bats were any indication.

"Well," King said at length, "I've got only two matches left and your light is dimming, Key."

"I'm going to light one of the two matches now," he said. "We've got to get out of here soon or else—"

He struck the match and let the draft blow it, shielding it with his hands while they went on. But it went out and his foot slipped. The flashlight in his hand smacked against the stony floor and also went out.

"Of all the dumb tricks," King growled. "And Doctor, I guess we'll have to use your light."

"Such as it is," said the Doctor.

Then he handed it over. King snapped the button and when he saw that the way was clear, he snapped it off again so that he could save the battery.

They moved on in pitch darkness now, feeling their way. Fifteen feet ahead he snapped the light on again for a moment.

It showed them a maze of corridors for what seemed the thousandth time. They stumbled on toward them.

"Sure none of the rest of you have any matches?" King said.

"Not me," said Shakespeare.

"Gee," said the Key, "what am I going to do for a smoke when I get out?"

"How are we going to get out?" the Doctor boomed. "That's what I want to know."

"We'll get out. Never fear," said the Bishop encouragingly.

King was grateful for that. Somehow it gave him more assurance just to hear the Bishop say that, and he knew, even if he could not see him in the dark, that his eyes were twinkling.

"Well, here goes," he said.

He struck the match. It flared. He held it up. The draft was coming from the corridor to the right.

"Well, I suppose this is the way we go," King said.

They started off. The Doctor's flashlight was very dim now. The only light left to them. King was saving it, flashing it on just an instant to see ahead, and then moving on cautiously in the darkness.

He was trying his best to think. Trying to figure some way that he might determine which way the draft blew without using a match. They reached the branching of the ways and stopped.

"You know," he said, "We've worked a stunt sometimes in the old barnstorming days when the air was pretty dead and we wanted to find out which way the wind was blowing if any. We stuck our finger in our mouth and wet it and then held it up over our heads and the cooler side of our finger indicated the direction of the wind. I wonder if it will work here or if it is too cold."

He pushed the button of the flashlight again to make sure of the passageways. The light refused to go on. It was done.

CHAPTER 13
FINGER OF HOPE

KING'S VOICE echoed through the caverns hollowly. "Well," he said, "that's that. I've heard something about the light that failed, but I never knew before just exactly what it meant."

He flung the light away from him with disgust and it crashed with a ghastly metallic sound against the rocks at their feet.

"We'll have to go on by sense of feel now," he said. "And let's hope we don't come to one of those bottomless pits. We'd better stretch out in a line and hold each other by the hand. I know certainly, from my standpoint anyway, there wouldn't be much glory in just dropping off into the bottom of the earth. And I imagine, Bishop, you and the rest of the band had better do a bit of silent praying on the side, for if this finger stunt doesn't work, we're sunk plenty."

"Yes," said the Bishop solemnly. "Perhaps it would be well."

King paused for an instant then he wet his index finger between his lips and held it up like a candle above his head. He tensed there a moment.

Every sense of feeling in his body seemed to be centered on that wet finger above him. Then he felt it. There was a cooling

135

sensation on the right side of the finger. He remembered when last the light had been on that there had been a corridor running in that direction.

"I think it worked," he exulted. "Let's go now. Luga you hold on to my left hand and each of you join hands behind him. Here we go."

Feeling his way with his free right hand King moved on very slowly, step by step. His hand touched stone. He moved away. He couldn't see now where corridors met and joined. He stubbed his toe on the sloping bottom of a stalagmite and at the same time his outstretched hand touched the stalactite above it.

"Hold it," he said. "I've got to wet my finger again. We're at another switch."

Then the Key piped up.

"Just so you take the right switches, fella," he yelled, "but don't forget if you holler 'end of the line, all out' I'm going to die of heart failure or somethin'."

King wet his finger and held it up. He couldn't see the passages before him. All he could do was follow the direction of the very gentle draft. He turned that way. The others followed. He found that way clear.

Something fluttered in front of him—a big bat. He took a sock at it with his open hand. It ducked and flew away.

"What was that?" demanded Shakespeare.

"Just a friendly little bat trying to take a nip out of my nose," King said.

He pushed on. Again and again he worked that wet finger stunt, found the way of the breeze and let the other members of

136

his Secret 6 band behind him. Then suddenly his outstretched right hand came in contact with a blank wall. He stopped there.

"Hold it," he cried. "We're up a blind alley."

He wet his finger and held it up again.

"No," he said. "We turn to the left here. That's a little bit better. We've been going to the right too much."

He made the turn and started on. Suddenly his feet slipped out from under him as though he had stepped on ice. He let out a wild cry.

"Hold it."

He felt Luga's great hand tighten instantly about his, felt himself jerked back as he felt his whole body seem to fly into space. He felt the strong arms of Luga about him lifting him up and standing him on his feet.

"Whew!" King exclaimed.

"Was it a bat?" asked the Doctor from the other end of the line.

"I haven't the slightest idea," said King. "All I can say is it's just like falling into a huge bottle of ink, only it isn't wet and the bottle has no bottom. Just a minute, Luga, we'll try it over to the left."

Inch by inch he moved on feeling with his right that was ahead. He struck firmer footing. It was level there. He put his weight on his right foot.

"Come on ahead now, one step. Hang on Luga and I'll try it again."

Now his groping right hand touched a cold clammy wall at

He felt Luga's great
hands tighten about
him, pull him back.

his left side. He kept as close to the wall as he could and moved his right foot ahead again.

"All right, now another step ahead. Come on, here we go—and keep as much to the left as you can."

They went on inch by inch, keeping as far away as possible from the great void that had tried to swallow up King. They moved for minutes that seemed like hours. Then King felt by groping about him that there was firm footing all along the passage and that the clammy stone walls were on either side of them. He stopped to take his bearing. Yes, the direction lay straight ahead.

His feet continued to touch solid rock on the floor. On and on they went. No more pitfalls. The corridor was long—longer than any they had gone through yet. He kept dragging his hand on the right side wall. It was as though the place had been hewn out by man. Then the wall fell away and they came to a turn. The shock of what he saw around that turn was almost too much, and the joy of it nearly overwhelmed him for the first second. He saw light shining very dimly—but light it was. It was reflected against the wall from some other point beyond.

EVERYONE SEEMED to see this at the same time. They were running, stumbling and sliding as they went for the next turn. King reached it and went around it like a flash and there before him he saw the entrance to the cave.

The light blinded them but they rushed on. Then they were outside by the embankment that led to the mouth of the mine entrance. It was as though the dread horror of being lost in those caverns was a great monster still pursuing them. They stopped to catch their breath.

"Jolly!" exclaimed the Bishop, still panting. "I'll tell you honestly, gentlemen, I never expected to get out of that place alive."

King laughed with relief.

"There's one thing certain, Bishop," he said, "the chances are if you didn't get out of there alive you'd never get out of there at all, because I don't think anybody would ever have found your body."

"You certainly don't mean, King, that you think the two giants are in there still?"

"To tell the truth," King said, "I don't think one way or the other about the giants. That's the most enormous cave I have ever seen or heard of. I'll bet there are very few people on Long Island that even know that it's there. Some enterprising promoter could make a barrel of money lighting that place up and charging a dollar a head."

King turned to Luga.

"There's one way of finding out more definitely about those giants," he said. "Suppose we scatter out and take a circle around this quarry and see if we can find some tracks that lead out in some other direction. If we find the tracks of the two giants we'll know that they aren't in the caverns yet. I certainly would have done that before if I'd had any idea of the cave's size."

"Hey," yelled the Key. "When do we eat?"

The Doctor looked at the little fellow with the twisted nose and laughed.

"From the looks of you it doesn't seem that eating ever did you any good anyway. What do you want to eat for?"

"Well, anyway, Doctor," Key observed, "I won't ever have a belly like a congressman, and I'll bet that's more than you can say."

"Come on," said King. "Let's spread out and start hunting." The six spread out over a wide area, climbed the sides of the quarry and began scouring the grounds about it. Each took a certain area and searched it for tracks.

Minutes passed. Luga was covering a wide area with great strides.

King looked up from his search just in time to see the big black stop short. Then he heard him call.

"Master, they go this way."

"What do you mean—both of them?" King inquired.

"No, master, just one. Luga mean both tracks. See here in grass."

King reached the spot and stared. Luga was right. He could see places where the grass had been trodden down in spaces eight or ten feet apart.

"Which one you think it is," asked Luga, "big giant or little giant!"

By now the others came running.

"Can't tell yet in this grass," said King. "Let's wait until we find the tracks in some soft earth. Then we can measure it and tell."

They trailed on with Luga in the lead. The giant tracks led across fields and over stone walls where they could see that the giant had stepped over without any trouble. They crossed a pasture and entered the wood lot of a farm. King looked about for the house and couldn't find it. It was probably behind a hill somewhere.

Then suddenly the tracks seemed to beat down the earth in a circle about the pasture. King frowned as they followed them.

"That's a funny thing," he said. "Here at this point the giant seemed to be chasing something."

They broke off in a straight stretch again.

"Well, he must have caught the thing pretty quick," said the Key, "because here he goes on."

King surveyed the pasture. In one corner of it he saw several head of cattle. They were fairly stampeding at sight of them.

"Look at those cows over there. They're scared green of us."

"Maybe," said Luga, "we find answer in woods."

THEY KEPT on the trail as it entered the woods. Then perhaps a hundred and fifty feet from the edge of the wood lot they came upon something. It was the body of a well-grown calf horribly torn apart. The Doctor bent down and examined the animal, what was left of it. He moved the head.

"The giant must have broken its neck," he said. "And that's no mean job. Looks like he tore the thing limb from limb. Must have eaten it raw."

"Jolly!" breathed the Bishop. "What brute strength."

"Believe me," said the Key, "that guy was hungry and so am I."

"Take another tuck in your belt," urged the Doctor, "That'll help if nothing else will."

They got up and moved on.

"Funny thing about this," King observed. "There is only one set of tracks. It looks to me that they are the tracks of the bigger giant. In that case where did the other go?"

They came upon a stream of water trickling down through a field beyond the wood. And in the soft earth beside the stream they saw not only the marks of the feet but also of the hands of the giant. Enormous hands they were, measuring two feet across as they stretched out. King unrolled his rule and measured the footprint. A blank look came over his face.

"Forty-two inches," he said. "This is the big fellow, all right. But how do you account for that extra inch, Doctor?"

"That's quite easy," said the Doctor. "This footprint is in mud. Of course it would sink down much deeper than it would in just the loose earth."

"Yes, I suppose that's true," King speculated. "Then what's become of the smaller giant, the one with the feet thirty-five inches long?"

The Doctor shook his head.

"Don't look at me," he said. "I haven't got him hidden away under my coat."

King glanced at the sun and then at his watch.

"Key," he observed, "I don't know but what you're right about eating. I'm getting hungry myself and it's useless trailing a giant that's got about eight hours start on us. I think I've got this position marked on my mind on Long Island and it might be possible to slow down our plane tomorrow morning and follow these tracks. Certainly a man of his size can't hide for long. What we've got to do is to try and find him and stop him before he starts on a wholesale murder campaign. Even if we start back for the car it will be very close to dark before we reach the cabin and there isn't a chance of catching him this way before night."

"Boy," cried the Key, "That's the first sensible thing you've said all day long."

The Key started off the way that they had come and the rest followed him wearily. It was along the creek back to the car when they passed the open hole in the side-hill of the quarry, King shook his head.

"You know," he said, "that cave ought to be walled up so poor ignoramuses like us wouldn't be apt to get lost in it."

"Yeah," rejoined the Key, "but wouldn't it have been funny if they had walled it up while we were in there trying to get out."

They finally reached the car as it was getting dusk. The Bishop dropped his ponderous weight into the back seat.

"Jolly!" he said, "it does seem awfully good to sit down for once."

"It'll seem awfully good," the Key grinned, "to sit down to Luga's cooking. I can tell you that much, Bishop. Every time I lose my appetite after this I'm going to think of today. Don't you forget it."

King took the wheel, turned the car around and then swung on to the main highway to the east. They whirled along at top speed through the dusk. It was getting cool as fall evenings will.

"I wonder," King resumed, as they swung into the bed-rock drive of the secret hideout, "how much we have missed on the short-wave radio by being away."

"I don't imagine," said the Bishop, "that we've missed a great deal. At least we can be sure that we have been on the trail of the giant marauders. I don't believe they've been able to do a great deal of damage out here in the open country. You notice that they—"

"He," corrected the Key.

The Bishop looked at him sharply.

"Why do you say he?" he asked.

"Well, of course, we found that footprints of two of them down there in the quarry," he said, "but you're talking about trailing *these guys* and we haven't been trailing *them*. We've been trailing *him*. First we trailed the guy with the thirty-five inch feet from Pennington's joint and after we left the quarry we trailed the old grand-dad mug with the forty-one inch feet or the forty-two inch ones, whichever you want."

"Very well," the Bishop said, "I'll alter my statement then. As I was about to say you notice that he seems to keep to the back country. All the time that we followed the tracks of the larger giant, they never once came near a house."

They parked the car and got out, walked wearily to the cabin that was hidden in the trees on the north shore. Luga hurriedly prepared the only meal for that day. The minute they got into the cabin the Doctor adjusted the shortwave receiver so that it would catch any message that might be sent.

"I'll tell you what I'd like to see," he boomed. "I'd like to see a fight between this forty-two-inch-foot giant and a full grown rhinoceros. Man, oh, man, would that be somethin'."

"Holy Gee," howled the Key. "With a show like that you'd bust the gate records of any fight ever promoted."

King was thoughtfully smoking and staring into the blaze he had started in the fireplace. For a long time he didn't say a word. Then he snapped his cigarette butt into the fire and said, "It may sound awful crazy but I'd like to have that picture in the District Attorney's office that has Henry Gilson in it."

"What in the name of time would you do with that?" demanded the Doctor.

King shrugged and smiled a little.

"I'm just working on the craziest hunch that a man ever had and I'm feeling very foolish even thinking of such a thing. So foolish, in fact, that I wouldn't even tell anyone what the hunch was."

The big Zulu chief bowed.

"Supper ready," he said.

There was a scramble for the seats at the table. They sat down and ate hungrily, finished and sat back and lighted their cigars and cigarettes. The Bishop filled his great Meerschaum pipe.

Then suddenly the shortwave radio began a low whistling sound and a voice was speaking to them.

"Hello, Secret 6! Hello, Secret 6! This is Legs Larkin speaking. I got some dope. Hope you're there to get it. My daughter went back to Pennington's place this morning to go to work again. Pennington just had her call up and tell me to get in touch with you guys and tell you he just got a message from the giant. The giant called him up on the telephone and the queer part of it is that he ain't askin' for any money. He's got somethin's else that he wants. Wants him to have a certain Doctor up at his place. The giant says he'll call up later and find out if he's got him. Pennington wants to see you up there right away. Guess he's about nuts."

King stared blankly at the radio. Legs Larkin's voice had stopped for a moment. Then it came in again.

"Pennington wants to see you guys as soon as you can get there. Get the idea? Can you hear me? I hope so. This is Legs signin' off now."

The radio went dead. King got up and reached for his coat. He glanced about the room. There were only five men there including himself.

"Let's go," he said. "I'm mighty glad we came back in time for that message."

He frowned as he stared about.

"Where's the Key?" he asked. "He was here a minute ago."

"Maybe he just stepped outside," the Bishop twinkled.

"All right. Come on," King said. "We're going to Pennington's just as fast as we can get there. The giant wanting Pennington to get a certain doctor up at his house is the funniest thing I've heard of in my life—as if the giant needed a doctor."

It was dark when they went out of the cabin.

King called, "Hey, Key, Key," but only the echo of his voice came back through the trees. They hurried to the place where the cars were kept. Each man was equipped with a fresh flashlight from the storeroom of the cabin, and in the light of his beam King stared at the place where the roadster had been.

"What goes on here," he demanded. "The roadster is gone and so is the Key."

CHAPTER 14
THE GIANT CALLS

"WHY, I can't understand it," exclaimed the Bishop. "It doesn't seem possible that the Key would go off on some mission without telling us."

"I don't know about that," the Doctor smiled. "Perhaps, Bishop, you remember another case when he disappeared. My only hope is that he can do as much good as he did then."

The Bishop laughed.

"You mean when he took the radio sets right out from under our noses and handed them out to his beggar friends?"

"Yes, that's it," agreed the Doctor. "You can't deny that move has helped a great deal. As a matter of fact, we couldn't have worked out some of these cases without the help of the Whistler, the Dummy, the Worm, or Legs Larkin or Flo the Fleecer."

"That's plenty true," said King, "but I can't for the life of me figure out what job the Key would be on tonight."

The Bishop smiled as he climbed into the rear seat of the sedan. "Probably some mission that he was afraid we wouldn't consent to."

King slid behind the wheel. Luga climbed in the front seat beside him. The Doctor, Shakespeare and the Bishop sat behind. The car backed out of the bushes, rolled down the bed-rock drive and presently turned onto the main highway heading west.

For almost an hour they sped on without speaking. It was totally dark. The traffic grew heavier as they reached the more thickly populated area of Long Island. Then they swung off the main highway toward the Pennington estate. This time King didn't drive past.

He pulled into the drive, followed it to the rear of the house. The door of the great stable and garage was open. He drove in as someone ran toward them across the lawn. The man—who was dressed in butler's uniform—bowed when he reached them.

"You're the gentlemen Mr. Pennington wished to see?"

"Yes," King answered sharply.

"Very well," said the butler, "please hurry. He's waiting for you in the living room. It's all very strange, sir."

"You're telling us," King laughed.

The butler led them around the house to the front. On entering the front door they found Mr. Pennington, not in the living room, but pacing the hall. He came over instantly and shook King's hand as though he were a long lost friend. King introduced the other members of his band.

"I'm sorry that the Key has disappeared. You'd enjoy meeting him."

"Disappeared!" said Pennington. "You mean the giant—"

"No," said King. "At least I don't think so. He's taken the car and gone somewhere without saying a word to any of us."

The Doctor spoke up then.

"Do I understand Mr. Pennington," he asked, "that the giant has 'phoned and asked to have a doctor here?"

Pennington nodded.

"In a way that's what happened. Let's go into the living room where we can sit down and be comfortable."

They went in and took chairs. Pennington didn't seem to

be so frightened tonight. As a fact, it seemed to be, more than anything, restlessness that was making him move about. He passed cigars and cigarettes to the five members of the Secret 6 and helped them light up, and then he lighted a cigar himself, went over and stood in front of the fireplace from where he faced them all.

"I'm very glad you've come," he said. "I feared perhaps you would be out and wouldn't get the message that I asked our first maid to have her father send you."

King said, "You seem much more at ease tonight than you did last night, Mr. Pennington."

"Strange to say, I am," said Pennington. "I don't know just how to express it. Perhaps it's because of a feeling that I'm more on the inside than I was. Last night I was the subject of blackmail. I was willing to pay for silence but after finding that note signed the Giant and then, of course, you know how the giant himself killed all four of the cutthroats who came to carry out the blackmail plot."

"By the way," King said, "I was going to ask you. Have the police bothered you about the accident down the road?"

Pennington smiled slightly. "The fact of the matter is," he said, "I haven't seen the police since they were here last night. It was a very clever trick of yours, King, to turn suspicion away from my household."

"I suppose," King grinned, "that you gave the lawn a good watering where the drive turns in to your estate?"

"Yes," Pennington said. "A very good watering. I'm sure anyone would have to dig for evidence of blood now. But to go on with what's happened tonight. I got a message direct from the giant himself."

"That's interesting," said King. "How can you be positive, though?"

"WELL, YOU see," Pennington went on, "the giant called me on the telephone. I've never heard his voice but I knew it was he. It was very deep and its timbre reminded me of thunder. It was as though some radio expert had taken an almost inaudible bass whisper and amplified it about ten times."

"And you say," King asked, "that he wanted you to get a doctor here. Some particular doctor?"

"Yes," Pennington nodded. "Doctor Rhinehart. The giant gave me his address in New York City. I've never heard of him. Perhaps some of you gentlemen have. How about you, Doctor?"

"Rhinehart," exclaimed King, "why he was the doctor who was whistling to his dog."

Then all eyes turned on the Doctor. He was studying a figure in the oriental rug at his feet.

"Rhinehart," he repeated. "Rhinehart."

"Yes," said Pennington, "Doctor F. C. Rhinehart. He lives at 609 West 76th Street. I don't know whether that's his office address or his home address. It may be both."

"That's odd," ruminated the Doctor. "The name sounds familiar. F. C. Rhinehart! Doctor F. C. Rhinehart. I can't seem to place him."

"It was Doctor Rhinehart who came whistling to those giant dogs. I'm sure of it now," King cried.

"I mean Doctor Rhinehart's name sounds familiar now—professionally," the Doctor exclaimed.

King turned to Pennington. "Exactly what did the giant say and when did he call?"

Pennington looked at his watch.

"He called about two hours ago. No, it was three hours ago approximately. The butler said a man with a most peculiar voice wanted to talk to me on the 'phone. When I answered the giant asked, 'is this Pennington?' I told him it was and instantly I had a very strange suspicion that the giant was talking. The next second he told me he was the giant. I remember that my hand shook so that I almost dropped the receiver. Then strangely enough, curiosity took the place of fear when I heard the next words.

"He said he didn't want money, that money wouldn't do him any good now. He wanted Doctor F. C. Rhinehart of 609 West 76th Street. He told me if I valued my life to have Doctor Rhinehart here as soon as I could get him and to have him come prepared to operate."

King leaned forward anxiously as a thought popped into his head.

"Did he say where to get in touch with him if you found the doctor?"

"No," said Pennington. "He said he'd call back later and he also finished by saying that if I called in the police, my life wouldn't be worth anything."

"And you haven't called in the police, of course," King asked.

"Certainly not," said Pennington, "at least not when I was quite sure I could get you of the Secret 6 to come."

Shakespeare was wagging his head.

"Most amazing! Most amazing!" he exclaimed softly.

"Yes indeed," said the Bishop. "It's a most interesting case, isn't it, Doctor?"

The Doctor half smiled. "I'm forced to admit it's a real case, all right," he said. "The strangest thing to me is the money. You say that the giant said money wouldn't be any good to him?"

"That's exactly what he said," said Pennington. "He said, 'money is no good to me now.' Apparently what the giant needs is a doctor."

"Maybe," ventured Luga, "big giant sick and want doctor."

"If that's the case," agreed the Doctor, "it's a very strange thing that he would have, what you might call, a family physician." He turned to Pennington. "Do you know, Pennington, that we have come to the conclusion that there are at least two and possibly three of these giants running about loose. Like that horde of giant dogs that was shot in New York."

Pennington's face whitened.

"Great Scott!"

King nodded. "One man," he said, "about seven feet tall, was seen coming out of Mark Fiddler's apartment two nights ago."

"Was that the same one," asked Pennington, "who came here last night, tipped over Fiddler's car and killed him and his three men?"

"I imagine that was another giant," King told him gravely.

"We trailed him to an old quarry way back in the center of

Long Island and there it appeared that he had met another giant. We found two pairs of footprints. One measured forty-one or possible forty-two inches long, and the other measured thirty-five inches. The smaller man was the one we trailed from your place."

Mr. Pennington took a long breath and uttered a very faint groan as he exhaled. He shook his head.

"I'm frank to admit, gentlemen," he said, "that if it were possible to follow this case from the side lines, I would enjoy it immensely. As it is, it's rather unnerving."

"I can understand that easily enough," said King. "Has the giant called you since?"

Pennington shook his head.

"Have you tried to get the doctor?" King asked.

Pennington shook his head again. "I haven't done anything on the case. I didn't want to until you gentlemen came. That's why I was in such a hurry to get you here. Do you think I should call the doctor?"

"I THINK," said King, "it will clear matters up a great deal. Suppose I try to get him."

He was sitting near a telephone stand at the side of the room when he spoke.

Lifting the receiver he asked for long distance.

"This is long distance," came in answer a moment later.

"Operator, I'd like to speak to Doctor F. C. Rhinehart of 609 West 76th Street."

"Who is calling," asked the girl.

"Mr. Pennington."

He waited a long time for an answer. He heard hummings and buzzings, broken bits of other conversations. At length the operator said: "I'm sorry but no one answers. Shall I repeat the call in a little while?"

"If you will, please," said King, "and ring me back if you get anything. Thank you." He hung up. "Well, the good Doctor F. C. Rhinehart seems to be out or asleep. Nobody home."

Pennington stared at him.

"What'll we do?" he asked. "Suppose the giant calls. What'll we tell him?"

King shrugged. "We'll tell him that we tried to get the doctor and he isn't in and try again. That's all we can do."

But King didn't leave the 'phone. He stayed there and called Flo. A few minutes later he heard her voice.

"Well," she laughed gaily, "this is certainly a pleasant surprise. What's on your mind tonight? I suppose it would be too much to hope that you called me up just to have a pleasant visit."

"Now, I ask you," King said, "is that nice?"

"I can't think of anything nicer."

"Listen," said King. "This is really serious. I want to ask you a question and then I'd like to have you do something for me."

"Very well," said Flo, "anything you say."

"About that big fellow you say you saw coming out of Mark Fiddler's place night before last. Did you notice his feet particularly?"

The girl's laugh came back at him over the 'phone.

"Now really, King, I'm not exactly what you might call a

connoisseur of feet. He wasn't pigeon-toed, I don't believe, if that's what you mean."

"No, no," said King. "What I mean is if he had feet about as long as a yardstick, you would have noticed, wouldn't you?"

"Good heavens, yes," exclaimed the girl. "I'm sure his feet weren't that long."

"Of course," said King, "then that confirms one suspicion. There are at least three giants in on this affair. The one who beat up Mark Fiddler, the one that we trailed last night with feet thirty-five inches long, and another one with feet six inches longer than that."

He heard Flo mumbling to herself on the other end of the line.

"Thirty-five and six makes forty-one. Good heavens, King, you don't mean any human has feet forty-one inches long?"

King had to laugh.

"As a matter of fact," he chuckled, "when he made that footprint he must have had his toes pulled up a bit for we measured another one and it measured forty-two. And now listen, something has happened tonight. One of these big men who calls himself the Giant has 'phoned up Mr. Pennington here at Glen Cove."

"Not *the* Mr. Pennington of Glen Cove?" Flo echoed.

"Right. I'm here now. The giant told Mr. Pennington if he knew what was good for him he'd call Doctor F. C. Rhinehart of 609 West 76th Street and have him come out to his house prepared to operate. Well, here's the hitch. I called the doctor and no one answers over there. I'm wondering if you won't hop in a cab and run over there, Flo. Find out all, where the doctor has gone and where he might be found. Then call me back here at Glen Cove 3490. Have you got that now?"

"I'm practically on my way," said Flo. "Oh, by the way, King, I just found out a little while ago that I made a mistake in the time Gladys and I saw the large man leaving Mark Fiddler's apartment. I told you it was eleven o'clock. But it might have been two or three hours later. Gladys' clock had stopped at eleven. Something is wrong with it and she has taken it |to the jewelers. I'm sorry if that upsets any of your theories."

"Thanks for telling me," King said. "Call me as soon as you have any news of Doctor Rhinehart."

"I surely will," the girl promised.

He hung up the 'phone and turned to the others.

"Flo says she just learned that it might have been one or two hours past midnight when she saw the big man leave Fiddler's apartment. I can't see how that alters the situation much, though. It still appears evident that there are three or four giants—that is including the smallest one who was just a little over six feet."

The telephone at his elbow jangled. He picked it up, said, "Hello."

A DEEP resonant voice came back over the wire. "Is this you, Pennington?"

King hesitated for a split second. "Yes," he said finally. "This is the giant?"

"It is," acknowledged the deep voice. "Have you got the doctor there?"

"Not yet," said King. "I've called him and he doesn't answer. I've sent a friend to get information on his whereabouts."

There was a pause. The giant's soft voice suddenly rose to a roar—it came so loud that King had all he could do to catch the words.

"Look here, Pennington," the giant bellowed, "if you're trying to kid me, I'll kill you. I tell you I've got to see Doctor Rhinehart before this thing goes any further."

"What thing?" asked King. "We're doing our best."

"That's none of your business."

"Where are you calling from?" King asked. "I'll call you back as soon as we have any word from the doctor."

"That isn't any of your business, either," bellowed the giant. "I'll get in touch with you. In fact, I think I'll start over there right now."

King tensed. "That'll be fine," he said, "then you can call the doctor yourself."

"I'll be there," said the giant. "If I find you've been trying to make a joke out of me I'll kill you and if you've called the police in on the case, I'll kill them too."

Then there was a loud click as the receiver was slammed on the hook at the other end. King shrugged.

"Well, I guess that's that," he said. "Nice gentle fellow, this giant."

Pennington was leaning forward eagerly in his chair.

"What did he say?" he asked a little shakily.

"He says he's coming over here," King said.

Pennington's face went white. "Coming from where?" he asked.

King shrugged. "I tried to find that out and he told me it was none of my business. And I don't suppose it is."

"But, great heavens," cried Pennington, "we can't have him coming in here. Why, a giant brute like that would kill all of us if he takes it into his head."

"We'll see," said King. "We're all fairly well armed. I don't know just how much effect bullets will have on a man of his size but I know there's one thing that seems very peculiar to me. If this giant went to school, the story certainly would have been in the papers, and at least one of us would have read it."

"What makes you think he went to school?" asked Shakespeare.

"Because he uses very good English."

The 'phone rang again. He took it. "Hello."

"King," said a girl's voice. "Doctor F.C. Rhinehart is out of town on a special case. He's at the Hospital for Aged in Chicago and is expected to be there several days. Is that any help?"

"I think it will be," said King. "Thanks a lot, Flo."

Then he hung up.

"Well, gentlemen," he said, turning, "that's that. Doctor Rhinehart has gone to Chicago for a few days. He's at the Hospital for the Aged and isn't expected back real soon."

Pennington's face took on an ashen look. "Good heavens! The giant will be here any minute now. What will he say?"

"We'll probably know that presently," the Bishop said, but his eyes didn't twinkle as merrily as usual now.

CHAPTER 15
JAILBIRD

WHEN KING said that he would like to have that picture of Henry Gilson the Key smiled to himself. It would be a great joke to sneak out on them, get the picture and bring it back and present it to King. He began planning instantly how he would go about it. It would be a good joke on the District Attorney. While the D.A. and the whole police force were looking for Henry Gilson, to have someone steal Gilson's picture right off the wall!

The Key chuckled softly as he sat in the dark corner of the cabin. The food that Luga was preparing smelled good. Nothing could hire him to leave until he had had at least that one meal for the day.

He sat down with the others and ate hungrily. Then when they pushed back their chairs and continued to talk, the Key edged toward the cabin door.

At one point all eyes were turned on King at the end of the table. Already the Key had the latch lifted. He only had to open the door about eight inches to allow his slim body to slide through. He was outside, grinning broadly. He closed the door behind him without a sound, picked his way softly through the dark woods until he came to the place where the two cars were hidden in the brush.

He climbed in the roadster, slipped behind the wheel and started the engine. It purred softly with little noise. He backed it out and started slowly, silently out of the bed-rock drive toward the main high-way. Then he heard King's voice echo through the woods calling his name.

He laughed.

"I'll be back pretty soon," he said to himself.

He turned west on the main highway and started for the city. Now and then he jangled a small bunch of keys in his pocket.

"Boy," he said. "This is going to be a pipe. All I gotta do is walk up, open the door in the office, slip the picture out and get goin'. I ought to be back at the cabin by midnight."

He swung through Brooklyn, across the bridge and downtown. As always, the Key rather flinched at sight of each policeman as he drove on. And each time he passed a cop he grinned. It seemed to be another mile stone in his life passed.

His pulse was racing high as he thought of a chance to get back into his old life for a moment. There seemed to be a certain satisfaction in pitting your brains against the brains of the police and winning out easily and skillfully so that you could laugh at them later.

"Of course, this will go all right with the Bishop because he'll know that I'm really hooking something that will help the case. It ain't like I was lifting a flock of dough or jewelry or somethin'."

He drew up before the downtown building that housed the District Attorney's office. The block was deserted. He parked the big roadster several doors beyond and got out.

The first thing he did was to stroll completely around the block, taking his time and enjoying a cigarette while he did it. He passed one cop on the back street walking his beat. The cop looked across the street at him and the Key looked back but the cop didn't have any idea that he was being scrutinized. The Key grinned.

"It's going to be a pip," he said. "Boy, oh, boy! Won't the D.A. be mad! I'll bet he'll be madder than if somebody took ten bucks out of his pocket."

The Key reached the front of the building again, turned easily and trod up the steps. No one was in sight. A dim light burned in the entrance lobby. If any elevators were working they were in use now. That was good, the Key decided.

He knew the layout well, as he had been here before. He found the stairs and trotted up the steps, reaching the second floor where the office was, hid his hands in his pockets, one hand on the small string of skeleton keys.

"A pip," he said again, almost out loud.

He found the door leading to the waiting room. Several times he had waited in that room in years past, handcuffed to a cop or a detective.

"But that ain't goin' to be no more," he said to himself. "I'm straight from now on."

He listened with his keen ears for any sound of warning. Beyond the glass of the door, it was dark. A very dim light burned in the hallway. He tried the door without a sound. It was locked. That was to be expected. The small ring of keys came out of his pocket. He chose one and inserted it in the lock, jingled it gently. Then, as though magic, the bolt slid back.

He stopped again with the door open, to listen. Still there was no warning sound. He opened it just enough and slipped inside, closing it softly behind him. The light from the street outside shone in the room. This was going to be easy. He didn't even have to use a flashlight.

He was in the waiting room now with the rows of seats about it. He glanced about and grinned. He could remember almost every place where he had sat in years past, handcuffed to a cop.

He stepped without a sound to the door beyond which opened into the office of the old man who had worked there for years.

He tried to remember. Did they call him Pete or Mike or what was it? Probably he was the one who had talked to King; then that would be the room where the picture hung.

He tried the door; it was locked. A moment later, under the dexterous hands of the Key, the door opened and he slipped inside. That room, like the other, was lighted from the street lamps outside. He shot a quick glance about, found a picture on the wall over the old man's locked roll top desk.

He stared at the picture, picked it off the wall and held it in the light of a street lamp that shone through the window.

"Holy gee!" he whistled softly. "Can that little guy on the end be Henry Gilson? Why, he isn't bigger than a pint of cider. Gee, he's a cocky lookin' little guy, too. He looks as if he thought he owned the D.A.'s office."

He looked at the date, 1925. He unfastened the clasp at the back of the frame and took out the picture of the group. Now he had it out and was staring at it.

"Gee," he said, "I just thought of something else that'll be better. All that King wants is Gilson's picture. Now if I just cut Gilson's picture out with my knife and put the rest of it back in the frame, that'll burn 'em up more than if I took the whole picture."

His fingers, moved rapidly. He opened a small pocket knife and cut around the head and shoulders of the picture of Henry Gilson, lifting it out of the group. Then he slipped the picture in the back of his watch and snapped the case shut.

Next, he slid the group picture with the hole in it, back into the frame.

HE LIFTED it up to hang it on the wall and tensed there as a sound came to him; a sound of ominous warning. Voices were coming from the hallway—loud angry voices. The knob of the door that led to the waiting room rattled. Men were coming in. The Key's old instincts came back to him.

He finished hanging that picture on the wall so that it was straight. Even stopped long enough to grin at the hole where Gilson's head had been. Then he turned quickly toward an inner door. The men were already in the waiting room now.

"That's mighty funny," he heard one of them say. "I thought you locked this place up last night."

"Confound it!" said another one, "you can't seem to find anyone you can trust around here."

Key slipped through the inner door just as the outer door was opened.

"Hey, what goes on here," demanded a booming voice. "This inside door is unlocked, too."

"I can't figure that out either," blustered the other one who had apologized before. That would probably be the District Attorney, himself.

But why were they coming in at this hour of the night? Key was in a darker room now. He leaped across it to another door which led into a larger office. Lights went on in offices behind him as the group of men advanced. He had reached an office now where there was no exit.

The men were coming on, exclaiming loudly. Two of them were taking another to task for carelessness in his department and he, in turn, was both apologizing for and cursing the employees whom he couldn't trust to lock doors when they left the offices. And all of the time the Key was chuckling to himself, even in this corner office where the only exit was through the door he had entered.

The men hadn't quite reached the room yet. Then the light flashed on there and as it did the light shining through the door caught the Key struggling with the window. He strained with all his might. The window wouldn't budge. Leaping over a desk he attacked another one, found the same condition and went on to another. The only escape left. He could hear the men walking across the office outside.

Clump! Clump! Clump!

The Key strained with all his might at that last window. It was stuck. Probably they had been freshly painted and hadn't loosened yet. He felt a little stickiness on his hands. Yes, that was the answer. The paint, where it was thickest, had come off on his hands.

He leaped away from the window as a heavy hand was laid on the doorknob. There was only one place for him to hide now.

The opening of the desk that was left for the legs of the man who sat before it.

Key dove into that hole. He doubled up in there as far back as he could. He was trying to make himself smaller as the light, went on and flooded the room.

Then the voices grew louder and more derisive.

"We come here to map out a plan so that we can trap the Secret 6," one man said, "and we find the whole place wide open."

"A pretty rotten state of affairs," said another. "It isn't enough that a trusted employee steals some of your old records and starts one of the greatest blackmail scandals this section has ever seen. But now we come up here and find the whole place as open as a ball park with the fence blown down."

"Gentlemen," said the third member, "I hardly know what to say. I'm as much astonished as you are, as you may realize. Beginning tomorrow morning we'll have a house cleaning in here. You can rest assured."

"Well, I hope it will do some good," growled the first speaker.

"I'll guarantee that it will," said the man who seemed to be the District Attorney.

"Alright," said the first speaker, "now let's get on with our plans. We don't want to waste this entire evening. You say you think you have a plan whereby we can lay a trap that will catch the whole band of men known as the Secret 6. Is that right?"

"It is," answered the attorney. "Take chairs, gentlemen, and I'll sit here at my desk and try to explain it to you. We'll see what you think of it."

The Key heard the men sit down, saw the legs and the lower

part of the district attorney's body as he sat down in his chair. He smelled the odor of cigar smoke.

"Of course," the attorney began, "don't misunderstand me. I don't wish to cast any reflection on the department of police of the city. However, you gentlemen will have to admit that the Secret 6 made a laughing stock of you when their leader 'phoned and told you to go to Fiddler's house and arrest Fiddler."

"Yeah!" said one of the other two. "Well, Fiddler got his last night, didn't he? The state police found him and three of his gang dead in his car that had crashed into a tree."

"Exactly," said the attorney, "but did you read this evening's paper? They didn't seem to help the situation any when they hinted that it was perhaps through the efforts of the Secret 6 that Mark Fiddler, the blackmailer, had met his death.

"And you've got to admit that it does look as if they had their hand in it. As a matter of fact didn't the troopers report that they found the crescent and small circle which is the sign of the Secret 6, somewhere on the blood-smeared car of Fiddler?"

"Alright, alright," growled one of the other men. "You don't have to rub it in." And under the desk the Key was grinning because, although he had forgotten to tell King about it, he had been the one who had put the sign of the Secret 6 on the side of the car with his finger dipped in Mark Fiddler's blood.

"I just mentioned this, gentlemen," the attorney said, "so that you won't think that I'm at fault too much by comparison."

"Go on with your plan to frame the Secret 6," growled one of the other men.

"Very well," said the attorney, "and I'm not pinning a bunch

of raspberries on you men either when I repeat what you already know. There's a leak somewhere in the police depart-
ment. We're sure of that.
The Secret 6 have some way
of learning what goes on in
police circles."

The Key grinned again
under the desk. He knew
what that leak was. It was
the Dummy and they had
never suspected him. The
attorney was going on.

"The only way you can
stop the razzing you're
getting because of the
Secret 6 is to stop the
Secret 6 and I think I have
a plan that will work. We'll
let it be known that Horace
Mann's butler has confessed
knowing more than he
has told already about the
case, and that he's trying
to communicate with the
Secret 6. Make it seem as

The Key raised his hands slowly.

though the butler only has confidence in the Secret 6. See what I mean?"

"Say," said one of the others, "that's a good idea."

"We'll frame it so that every man on the force hears about it.

Whoever information is leaking through in the police department will inform the Secret 6 that the butler has something important to tell them. We'll have a guard of men around that banker's mansion all the time. And when the Secret 6 come to contact the butler, it's going to be just too bad."

THE KEY was growing more and more tense. It was very important that he learn all the details of this. As soon as he got free, he would get back to the Secret 6 and tell them what was up and what they could expect.

"Sounds good to me," said the other of the three. "We can start as soon as we get back to headquarters. Suppose you write out the scheme in detail, just so we have it all straight."

"I'll be glad to," said the attorney.

Then Key grew rigid under the desk. The Attorney was turning around. He was sliding his legs under the desk as he pushed his chair up to it. Before he had been sitting with his back to the desk.

Key heard a light pounding and a rustle of paper as the attorney prepared to write. The attorney's feet were moving forward. He kicked the Key in the ribs, kicked him harder and seemed to be pressing him with his foot.

"Confound it," he exclaimed. "What's under this desk, anyway? There isn't any room for my feet."

The Key moved as the attorney swung back his chair and bent over to peer inside the desk well. Then like a bolt of lightning, the Key charged out from under that desk. A loud exclamation sounded from the men. They leaped from their chairs. They were big powerful men, police officers of high rank.

They moved to close in on him. The Key dodged and shot to one side. Then the one nearest him jerked his hand out of a shoulder holster and in his hand came a police revolver.

"Go on. Run, you rat," he growled. "I'd take a lot of pleasure in drilling you and even if I was alone without witnesses, I don't know as I'd hesitate. It would save a lot of legal expenses."

The Key stood stock still. He raised his hands over his head. The big police officer was advancing toward him. The attorney and the other one were closing in from behind. They were running their hands softly over his clothing to make sure that he had no weapon concealed there. Then he stepped back away from the Key.

"Say," said the one, "you look an awful lot like the rat that escaped from the Death House some months ago. Are you?"

He jabbed him with his gun. The Key jumped.

"Me in the Death House! Don't make me laugh. Listen, mister, I never did nothin'. It got kind of chilly out doors and I came lookin' for a place to sleep."

"Come on, don't try to kid me," said the largest of the cops. "And I suppose you walked right into the District Attorney's office to find a place to sleep. Well, you'll sure get a bed for a long time and it won't cost you anything, either. If we find out by your fingerprints that you're the guy that was in the Death House and got out, there's going to be a lot of fun. You'll see the 'hot seat' this time and it'll be hot, too."

"No foolin'," the Key insisted, "Honest I ain't done nothin'. I'm telling you straight. I just came in here to get warm and find a place to sleep. I found all the doors open so I just walked right in."

"You hear that," said the police officer. "He found the doors open, attorney. Just walked in to get warm. What do you think of that?"

"Well, nobody will find them open after this," the attorney assured them, "I'll fire every man in the department if I have to, to get at the bottom of this."

"Wait a minute," said one of the cops, "let me look in those pockets again. Maybe there's some burglar's tools around here."

"If there was, I wouldn't know how to use them. You ought to know I was innocent just to look at my face."

And all of that time the Key was hoping that they wouldn't look under the desk because while he was there he had taken the keys noiselessly out of his pocket and shoved them between the desk and the floor in order to do away with any incriminating evidence.

The men ran through his pockets. One took his watch and looked at it.

"Where did you steal this?" he asked.

"That's a good one," grinned the Key. "You find a dollar watch in my pocket and then ask me where I stole it. That's hot, that is."

"All right. Shut up, you rat," growled the other police officer. "Come on, you're going with us."

They loaded him into a car that was standing in front of the office. As they passed the lonely roadster further down the block, the Key looked longingly at it. A few minutes later they drew up in front of police headquarters, took the Key inside.

"What's your name," asked the cop at the desk.

"Why should I tell you," snapped the Key. "A guy wouldn't get a square deal here anyway."

"Now listen," said the cop. "I'm going to ask you your name once more."

"It doesn't matter," said another cop, coming up from the rogue's gallery. "Here's his mug and his fingerprints, too. He's the guy that escaped from the Death House several months ago at the same time that the Bishop got King out. He's one of the Secret 6 gang."

The cop at the desk stared and blinked.

"Holy mackerel! That's him all right, isn't it?" He stared from the rogue's gallery photo to the Key's face and back again. "Say," he said turning to the other cop, "maybe this guy's the rat that they call the Key in the Secret 6."

The Key grinned. "I'd sure feel flattered to hear that. If I was hooked up to the Secret 6, I'd show some of you mugs how to solve crime."

"Shut up," cracked the cop. "Give me your hand. I want to test these finger prints."

He took the fingers, pressed them on an ink pad and then pressed them on blank sheets of paper. While the Key waited, they compared his prints with those below the rogue's gallery photo. Finally the sergeant shook his head.

"There's something funny here," he said. "This guy is sure the one that escaped out of the Death House all right, but his finger prints aren't the same."

He jerked his head back. "Well, stick him in the jug anyway, and lock him up good. The Secret 6 is a slippery outfit and here's one that isn't going to get away."

The Key was led back into a prison cell. The heavy door clanged shut on him and was locked.

CHAPTER 16
THE MONSTER SPEAKS

A T THAT very moment King and the remainder of his band were waiting in the living room of the Pennington mansion. Mr. Pennington had gotten up and was pacing the floor.

"Why doesn't something happen," he demanded at length.

"I'm just trying to think," King said, "what is the best thing to do. I feel well enough satisfied in my own mind that we have enough on this giant to justify shooting him on sight. I think the best idea would be for all of us to get outside. When he comes we can attack him and—"

He stopped suddenly. Everyone tensed as though the place had been charged with electricity.

Thud! Thud! The sound came from the front porch. A second later the doorbell jangled. King leaped to his feet, gun in hand.

"Wait," he said, "let me answer it."

He started for the door that led out into the hall and all eyes were focused on him. *Crrrrash!* The sound was deafening. King whirled, looked back at the living room. It was in a shambles. Two French doors were being torn out bodily, jams, casings and all. The whole outer wall was vanishing into splintering wood and falling plaster. Then a giant head and shoulders protruded inward, followed by a huge arm.

The men stood petrified.

"Drop your guns." His bellowing voice echoed through the house and seemed to make the great mansion shudder with the terrific volume.

"Don't move, any of you, or I'll kill you. Which one of you is Pennington?"

Pennington's lips moved, trembled. "I—I—I'm Pennington," he managed to get out.

The giant's face with its stubble growth of beard, turned toward him.

"I thought I told you not to call in the police," the monster roared.

"These are not the police," stammered Pennington. "They are friends of mine who happened to drop in to call this evening."

"Oh, I see," said the giant, "and they always carry guns when they come to call on you, do they?"

The giant made a horrible spectacle as he leered at them. He was so huge that he couldn't begin to stand up in the room. He was outside on the porch on his hands and knees and except for an old pair of trousers that were about his middle, more as a loin cloth than pants, he was stark naked.

He glared from one member of the Secret 6 to another. At any moment he might pull the trigger of that big revolver and spatter them with lead. But something seemed to change his mind. His eyes moved to Pennington again.

"Have you got the doctor," he demanded.

175

"I'm very sorry," said Pennington, "but he has gone to Chicago to the Hospital for the Aged."

"Gone," repeated the giant. His voice was shaky, almost like trembling thunder.

Everyone in the room stared at him, stared in amazement.

"Gone," he said again.

King spoke up then.

"We're very sorry for you, giant, if you're in trouble. We would like to do anything we could to help you out. There's a doctor in the room here, a very famous scientist and surgeon. He might be able to help you if you tell him what you wish."

The giant's head turned slowly on his huge shoulders and neck. The great eyes glared full at King.

"My reason for wanting a doctor is none of your business. It's no business of any of you. Do you think I want to be any more of a laughing stock than I am now?"

King shook his head. "I don't see anything particularly laughable about you. How tall are you?"

"Heaven only knows," grumbled the giant. "Too tall."

"Was it you," King asked, "who killed Mark Fiddler here last night?"

The giant nodded. It reminded one of a great oil drum or ball moving up and down. There must be something mechanical about this giant and yet he looked perfectly human. Also, there was something in that huge face that haunted King. Something that he couldn't get out of his mind. He was almost positive he had seen that face before.

"Yes," thundered the giant. "Certainly I killed Mark Fiddler and his cutthroats. He deserved to die. That's what started all the trouble."

"What trouble?" asked King, not unkindly.

"That's none of your business," bellowed the giant. "I'm here to get that doctor."

"I—I'm sorry," said Pennington, "but I—I—I told you he'll be in Chicago several days."

Then a frightened look came into the giant's face and eyes.

"I've got to get him quicker," he said. "That's too long."

"As I told you before," King said, "we've a doctor here in the room. I'll gamble that he can do as much for you as Doctor Rhinehart can."

The giant glanced at the Doctor with his great eyes narrowed.

"No," he said sadly, "there's only one doctor that can help me."

"Of course," King went on, "we're just friends of Mr. Pennington's who happened to drop in for the evening, but we're deeply interested, nevertheless. We've never heard of a man as large as you are."

"No," bellowed the giant, "and I hope to heaven you never will!"

All the time as he talked, the gun was waving around. Men tensed as it swung toward them, and then relaxed slightly as it turned toward others. But there seemed to be more fear than murder in the eyes of the giant.

"The whole thing seems so strange," King said. "Your voice and your looks don't seem like those of a killer. How did you happen to murder the old prospector down in the gypsum quarry?"

The giant hesitated as he swung his eyes toward him.

"Or," King corrected, "perhaps it was the other giant who was with you."

"The other giant!" he exclaimed. "Good heavens, are there two of us?"

King's mouth dropped open. "Aren't there," he asked.

The giant didn't answer; his great face had a puzzled expression.

"Sometimes I go mad in my condition. You've guessed correctly, young man, I'm not a killer, normally, but when I'm in one of these mad states I'll smash anything in my way. I remember now. I reached the quarry in the dark and had just started up toward the entrance of the old mine. The old prospector must have heard me. He came out of his shack demanding to know what I was doing there. He startled me and threw me into a temporary fit of insanity. I rushed back and murdered the poor old fellow."

His face darkened; his whole nature seemed to change suddenly.

"Get Doctor Rhinehart. If you don't have him within the next twenty-four hours I'll hunt you out and I'll kill you all. I'll kill everybody."

Then he withdrew from the gaping hole he had made in the side of the living room. They heard him thudding down off the porch; he took the steps in one great stride.

KING LEAPED through the hall door and rushed through, turning out the lights as he went. He tore out of the front door, his big automatic in his hand. Then he stood motionless for a moment, trying to listen while the others came pounding behind him with their guns in hand. They had picked them up where they had dropped them but the giant had already vanished.

"Listen," said King.

Thud! Thud! Thud!

They could hear the great pounding of the enormous feet as the giant ran far out of sight in the darkness. King listened until the heavy thumping had died away. It was like the steady beating of African signal drums. Drums that were sending a message of something that they did not know about or could not understand.

Thud! Thud! Thud!

When the sound came no more he turned and faced the men behind him.

"Well, gentlemen you've seen the giant. You've met him in person."

The Bishop was first to speak. "You know," he said, "this may sound strange but somehow I feel sorry for him."

"I can't help feeling a little sorry myself," said King.

"It's the strangest thing I've ever witnessed or read of. How tall would you say he was," the Doctor asked.

"Well, let's see," said King thoughtfully. He walked down the porch toward the debris-littered floor where the giant had torn half the side of the living room off.

"I'm not quite six feet tall," King said, "and there's room under this porch roof for a man to stand straight if he were twice as tall as I am and that would be nearly twelve feet, lacking an inch or two. You've very high ceilings, Mr. Pennington."

"Yes," said Mr. Pennington, "V-very high."

"The giant," said King, "was crouched just about here. I should say, and even so filled about seven or eight feet."

"That might mean," said Shakespeare, "that he was anywhere between fifteen and twenty feet tall."

"Impossible," bellowed the Doctor.

King shrugged. "Well, Doctor, you were standing right beside me where you could get a good look at him."

He stopped suddenly and stared down at his feet. In the light that blasted out of the hole in the living room wall, he saw something on the porch floor that looked like a small piece of leather material. Stooping, he picked it up. It was just that, a small leather billfold.

"Will you look at this," he exclaimed. "Here's a billfold, regular size. It apparently been dropped out of those trousers that the giant's wearing for a loin cloth. They're certainly far too small for him to wear as pants."

He opened the pocketbook, stared at the contents. The others crowded about him. There was no money in it but there were a few cards. He took them out and examined them. An exclamation of astonishment left his lips.

"This is the billfold of Henry Gilson!"

"That's odd, and yet not so odd as it might be," the Bishop cut in. "Didn't Mark Fiddler tell you that the man who had beat him up and who had taken the stolen records from him, was Henry Gilson."

"Yes," said King, "Of course, but that couldn't be. We established that after I got the news from the district attorney's office.

Gilson is only a little bit of a man. He can't compare with the man Flo says beat up Mark Fiddler."

"Perhaps," Shakespeare ventured, "this giant in some way procured Henry Gilson's—er trousers, pocketbook and all."

"Say that's an idea," said the Doctor. "Maybe this giant and Gilson are working together."

"And again," said the Bishop, "perhaps they're not. It may be that the giant has already killed Gilson."

"I don't think any of those things matter so particularly now," King said. "The main thing we've got to do is get this giant out of the way. Somehow he seems to think he will be perfectly normal if he can get hold of Doctor Rhinehart to operate. I don't know how shots would affect him. Ordinary bullets might bother him very little unless they hit a vital spot."

"I'll bet," the Doctor smiled, "that an old French seventy-five would finish him up in great style."

"Yes," King nodded, "I can imagine it would. But we haven't got the giant and we haven't got a seventy-five."

He was thoughtful for a moment as they walked back toward the entrance of the house. Then he turned quickly to Pennington. "Suppose you call the doctor, long distance on your telephone. He's at the Hospital for the Aged in Chicago. Tell him to meet me at the Chicago Municipal Airport at three o'clock tomorrow afternoon. On my way there I'll fly over your estate and if for any reason the doctor can't come, stake a sheet down in the middle of your lawn and I'll understand."

"I'll do it," said Pennington. "Suppose the giant should come back. What'll I tell him?"

"Exactly what we're doing," said King. "Tell him I'm flying out to Chicago to get the doctor."

"Very well," said Pennington. "But I can't see what earthly use it's going to be."

"It's just a feeling I have," said King, "not even a hunch. I have the feeling that if the doctor gets out here in time, the giant won't be dangerous any more. I can't explain it any further than that."

Then King nodded to his men.

"I think that we might as well go back to our headquarters. Any time you want us, Mr. Pennington, you know how to reach us through your first maid."

"Yes," said Pennington, "and rest assured, I'm grateful to you. I hope I can make it right with you some time."

King and the four other members of the Secret 6 walked off the porch and around back of the house to their car. They climbed in and drove off for the cabin.

That was a strange ride back. One would open his mouth to ask a question and then would close it before any words came out They were completely baffled and King was the most silent of the whole band. As they drove into the bedrock drive, King said: "I wonder if the Key is back yet."

But his expression of hope vanished as he drove into the place where the cars were usually hidden and found an empty space where the roadster should be.

"I wonder if anything has happened to the Key," he said.

"No doubt he's quite all right," said the Bishop. "He can take care of himself very well."

The moment they entered the cabin the Doctor stepped over to his shortwave radio receiver, turned it on. They heard a crackling, whistling sound at first, then a humming, then suddenly words were coming out at them. It was the dull monotone of the Dummy's voice.

The Dummy was saying, "—and they got him in jail down here in headquarters."

"What's that," demanded King. "They got the Key?"

"Listen," said the Doctor, "I think he's going to repeat."

The radio seemed to go dead. The sound faded and the whistling stopped. King stared at the radio.

"If we had been in here two or three minutes before we would have heard the whole thing. And we haven't any way of telling the Dummy that we didn't hear."

He lighted a cigarette and paced the floor. The others were standing or sitting, their hopes fading. Then suddenly a low hum and whistling started again and the steady monotone of the Dummy's voice came back.

"Hello, Secret 6. Hello, Secret 6. Want to be sure you get this. The butler at Horace Mann's has told the cops that he's got some information that he won't give to anybody else but the Secret 6. The cops are awful mad. They had him down and grilled him but it don't do any good. And here's some more news that ain't so good. They got the Key a little while ago up in the District Attorney's office. He was hidden under the District Attorney's desk. They've got him in the jug down here at headquarters."

CHAPTER 17
KING, POLICE
COMMISSIONER!

K ING GLANCED from the loud speaker of the radio to his men.

"The Key's in jail. Before we do anything else we've got to get him out. He may have learned something that will save us a lot of trouble."

The Doctor shot him a sarcastic glance.

"That's a clever thought," he said. "They've got the Key in jail at headquarters so we're supposed to march down there, hold up the whole police force and demand his release. Is that the idea?"

King laughed and shook his head.

"I'm afraid, Doctor, you're a little ahead of me. Let me think."

He lit a cigarette, glanced at his wrist watch and then he dropped into a chair and stared to the fireplace where Luga had just kindled a fire.

"Who it is," he said, "that the police at headquarters would have the most respect for?"

Several of the group opened their mouths but King interrupted them.

"Wait, now. Don't tell me. I've got my own ideas. If the Mayor and the Commissioner of Police were to walk in there together they would snap to it, wouldn't they?"

"Have you gone completely crazy?" demanded the Doctor.

King laughed.

"I don't think so," he said. "I think it will work all right. That is, Shakespeare, if you think you could do your work properly with the makeup kit."

Shakespeare's eye widened.

"Am I to understand," he said, "that you want me to make up two of you to represent the Mayor and the Police Commissioner?"

"Sure," said King. "We've got some pictures of them around here somewhere. Why not? I'll be the Police Commissioner and Bishop, you can be the Mayor."

The Doctor spoke and there was still a little sarcasm in his voice.

"How about me?" he asked. "Can't I play, too?"

"Not this time," said King with mock severity. "You've laughed at our game and made fun of it so I don't think you can play. You can go home and slide down your own cellar door. Come on; let's get out some pictures of the Mayor and the Commissioner so we can see what they look like. And Shakespeare you can get out your makeup kit and prepare to bring about the miraculous change."

As King said that he began stepping out of his clothes.

"I'll have to wear a darker suit as the Commissioner of Police." He looked at the Bishop and smiled. "You know, the more I look at you the more I realize that you're going to make a pretty good mayor. You and the Mayor have more in common than I realized."

"I hope," said the Bishop, "this will be a success."

"It's got to," said King.

Then they reclined, each in an easy chair. Shakespeare worked on them, beginning with King. He worked rapidly and deftly with skilled fingers. In a matter of ten or fifteen minutes, King had the distinguished appearance of the Police Commissioner. He had gray hair where it should be, features to match, lines where they appeared in the photograph of the Commissioner. He stepped before a small mirror on the wall.

"By George," exclaimed the Doctor, "I'll be honest with you. I didn't think it could be done."

King laughed. "How does my face wrinkle up? O.K.?"

"Excellent," said the Doctor. "I knew the Police Commissioner fairly well when I was over in France. The only thing you and the Bishop need is to pep up your conversation a little more and get it just a bit snappier to imitate their voices. You particularly, King. You've got to eliminate that slight drawl that you developed in the flying game when you lived south so much."

"Right," said King rapidly. "I'll do my very best. Is that better?"

"Much better," said the Doctor. "I think you've got it."

Shakespeare stepped away from the face of the Bishop and looked at him.

"I think, Bishop," he said, "that you'll make a very commendable Mayor. Yes, indeed, a very commendable one."

The Bishop got up now and looked into the mirror.

"Jolly," he said, "can this be me?"

"Forget it," said King. "From now on you're the Mayor and I'm the Commissioner and nobody is going to talk us out of it. Now, Bishop, a dark suit."

"Yes," said the Doctor, "and pull in your paunch a little bit so that you won't look quite so stout."

They hauled and tugged at the Bishop's vest, pinned it and strapped it in behind so that it would make his waist line smaller.

"Phew!" puffed the Bishop, "I don't know if I can hold this any too long or not but I'll try."

"We'll get it in shape," said King. "Then you can unbutton your vest and rest at ease, at least until we get down to headquarters. The Bishop unbuttoned his vest hurriedly.

"Jolly," he said, "that's better." His eyes twinkled. "It's almost worth standing the pressure in order to feel the relief that you get when you unbutton the vest." He turned to King. "Well, how do we go, just the two of us?"

King hesitated and a smile crept over his face.

"Doctor, I think you would make an excellent chauffeur. You have the distinguished look that should go with a chauffeur."

The Bishop shot a quizzical glance at the Doctor.

"I can't know," he said. "I'm tempted to disagree with you." He turned to Luga. "You drive the car, don't you, Luga?" he asked.

"Yes, Bishop, I drive," said Luga.

The Bishop's eyes twinkled again.

"What could be more fitting than a big colored chauffeur? We'll try to get him into one of my frock coats and put one of the Key's caps on his head and he ought to carry it off finely."

"Of course," said King, "I guess that lets you out Doctor. On second thought, perhaps you're a bit too distinguished looking. Maybe if anybody saw your powerful shoulders and that heavy neck of yours, they'd take you for a rather brainy gangster."

The Doctor shrugged. "At least I'm grateful for the brainy part of the compliment, anyway."

The Bishop got out one of his frock coats. It fitted Luga almost like a glove, but a bit sooner than that.

"Think you can drive all right without bursting it open?" the Bishop asked a bit fearfully.

"If Luga not have to fight," came back the reply, "Luga not break out coat."

"Let's hope you don't have to fight," said King, "but if you do it will be worth it. In that case we won't worry about the coat. Now are we ready?"

"You look," said Shakespeare, "as though you might be ready for anything that might come up. The Mayor and Police Commissioner of New York. I hope, gentlemen, you can act the parts."

"We'll do our darndest," King promised.

THEY WENT out, training their flashlights ahead of them, walked through the woods to the place where the sedan was hidden. Luga climbed into the front seat. King opened the rear door and stepped aside. He bowed with a gallant air.

"You first, my dear Mayor," he said.

"No, you first."

"No, you first," said King. "You see, my job depends on you."

"Very well," said the Bishop.

He climbed in and settled in the rear seat. King sat down beside him. The engine started. They were backing out. Then they were rolling along the bed-rock drive through the woods and turning into the main highway.

As Luga drove on the Bishop asked, "Now just what will we say to the police when we get there?"

"How's this for a story?" King asked. "We pull up in front of headquarters and walk right in as though we owned the place. Don't worry, any cops that we meet will give us the royal salute. We'll go right up to the desk Sergeant, tell him we understand that they've got a man who's suspected of being a member of the Secret 6 and demand to see him. Maybe you had better let me handle the conversation and back me up in anything I say. After all, I'm the Police Commissioner."

"Very well," said the Bishop.

"I'll try to cook up some special reason between now and the time we get there why we want to see him. When they bring him out we'll nod our heads and say that's the man we want. We'll order them to release him in our hands and we'll be responsible for a special secret reason."

"You think," demanded the Bishop, "that it's going to be as easy as that?"

"Well, if it isn't," King said, "we're going to have one sweet time getting him out. In any event, we might as well try the easiest way."

Luga drove on through Brooklyn, across the bridge and downtown in Manhattan. King and the Bishop lounged easily in the back seat but the nerves of each were a little taut for what was to come.

They reached the block where headquarters was located.

"Drive around the block once, Luga," King said, "so that we can get the lay of the land first."

They turned to come in front of the police headquarters. King watched as they passed. A cop was just coming out of the front door. Another was going in. He saw a dim light burning in the hall inside. He looked back as they went on. Another cop was going out.

"There'll be plenty of those inside," King observed. "The minute we get in the place they'll spread the news that we're coming. They'll be all waiting to receive the Mayor and Commissioner when we get there.

They rounded the block and came back.

"Now stop right out front of headquarters, Luga," King said.

"Yes, Master," said the big black.

The car slowed and swung to the curb. In the hall that they could see up the long steps inside the front doors, a cop was just coming out.

"Here's where we get a break," King whispered.

He reached and swung the door open. The Bishop was struggling to get his vest buttoned.

"Hurry up. Let's go."

"Wait a second until I get this top button fastened."

King was out ahead of him. Then the Bishop followed and Luga slammed the door shut and sat stiffly in his seat in the dark behind the wheel. A streetlight spread a dull glow over the faces and figures as the two trotted up the steps.

The police officer reached the door and glanced out. He saw them coming and turned quickly.

"Now the news spreads," King said.

They pulled the doors and strode inside and there was an air about them. They walked rapidly together. A cop stopped before them and stood at attention. They nodded as they passed but seemed to be very busily engaged in talking. Other policemen put in an appearance.

One came blinking his eyes, from a room at the side, pulling on his coat. All along cops snapped to attention as the Mayor and the Commissioner breezed in before them. The captain behind the desk rose and bowed.

"Good evening," he said, "this is certainly a pleasant surprise at this hour of the night, sir. It isn't often that we get the Mayor and the Commissioner at the same time well after midnight."

King smiled slightly.

"Keep your seat, captain," he said. "We're here on a little private investigation. We heard a short time ago that you had a young man whom you suspected of being connected with this organization known as—" He turned to the Bishop. "The Secret 6, isn't it?"

"Yes, Commissioner, that's right."

King glanced sharply at the captain. The room was rather dimly lighted and there was a light above the captain's desk that shone down on the top of them. It was shaded above and left the faces of both King and the Bishop in the shadow.

"You mean the little fellow we caught up in the District Attorney's office, Commissioner," said the captain.

"I believe that's the man," King said. "If you'll bring him out we can tell the moment we see him."

Instantly, the captain whirled in his chair.

"Flannigan, bring out the prisoner."

"Yes, sir," said Flannigan. He disappeared through a door.

King leaned a little closer to the captain with a confidential air.

"You see, captain," he said, "we've a special reason, the Mayor and I, for wanting this man. We will be responsible for him, of course."

"Well, of course," said the captain. "If you and the Mayor aren't responsible for him, who is I'd like to know."

The Bishop and King both smiled slightly but they didn't say anything to that. There was a sound of feet treading the corridor beyond the door. Then big burly Flannigan came in with the Key walking before him. The King and the Bishop both looked at him and he looked at them. It was plain to see that he didn't recognize them. He blinked at them and then at the captain behind the desk, then laughed at Flannigan.

"Say," he demanded, "what is this, a dream or somethin'? Ain't that the Mayor and the Commissioner? You say they come all the way over here to see me?"

"Shut up," barked Flannigan.

King squinted harder at the Key.

"That's the man, captain. We'll take him along."

"Just the two of you?" asked the captain.

King tensed a little. "Certainly," he said, with a little ice in his voice. "You think we can't handle a little rat like that?"

"Well, excuse me," blustered the captain. "I meant no offense at all. I only meant to say he's a dangerous character."

"We'll take care of him," said King.

"Yes," said the Bishop. "Don't worry. We're both armed."

"That's all right then," said the captain.

King jerked his head toward the Key.

"Come on," he said.

The Key started, got out near them and then hung back.

"Hey, wait a minute; you guys ain't going to take me for no ride, are you? I've heard somethin' about maybe you big shots was goin' to finish some of us guys that you couldn't get anything on any other way."

KING WHIRLED and grabbed the Key by one arm. The Bishop took his cue and grabbed him by the other arm. They half dragged, half walked him, still struggling between them, out of headquarters, down the steps and out to the sedan. Luga had the door open when they reached it.

The Bishop got in first then King shoved the Key in, but he didn't struggle so hard now, climbed in behind him and closed the door. Instantly the car shot in motion and rolled down the street.

"Why, what the hell," exploded the Key.

"Ah, ah, ah," said the Bishop.

"I mean what's going on here," the Key stammered. "Holy gee. I thought you guys were sure enough the Mayor and the Commissioner. Honest I did."

King laughed. "So did the men at headquarters," he said. "We're going uptown, Luga."

The car turned north.

"Say," the Key said suddenly beginning to wake up, "that was the slickest job I ever seen pulled. Holy gee, and I thought I was clever. You guys put it over them like a blanket of fog. Where you going now?"

"I don't know," said King. "It all depends on what you've got to offer. Why in the name of time would you come down here all alone and get into a jam like this anyway, Key?"

The Key grinned at them sheepishly.

"Well, here it is," he explained. "I heard you say you would give a lot to have that picture of Gilson that was in the group in the D.A.'s office."

"You didn't get it?" King exploded.

"You're darn right I got it," the Key said. "If I hadn't tried to be so funny I wouldn't be in the jug. I figured it would be a good joke on the D.A. and the whole gang if I just cut out the little guy and put the picture back in the frame. A gang came in cookin' up a deal to frame the Secret 6 while I was there. Can you imagine that? They cornered me. I hid under the D.A.'s desk but the D.A. found me when he started kicking around in there to get room for his feet. If I had just taken the whole picture and hadn't tried to be so funny, I'd have gotten out before they came in. I know da—darn well I would."

"What did you just say about a plot to frame the Secret 6," King demanded.

"Sure," said the Key, "they're after us. They'd give anything to get us. Hey, wait Luga, turn to the right here. I left the roadster down the street here. I'll drive it home if you don't want me anymore."

"Slow up, Luga," said King. "I want to hear about the trick the police think they're playing on us."

"It isn't a bad trick," said the Key. "The cops know that information has been leaking out of the offices and getting to us, but they don't know who's doing it."

"So they started the story," King said, "that the butler at Horace Mann's place had some important information which he would only hand out to the Secret 6. Is that what you mean?"

"That's it," said the Key. "How did you guess it?"

"We didn't have to guess it," said King. "The Dummy sent out the word. We'd have a tough time without the Dummy. Have you got that picture?"

"Sure," the Key said, fishing in his pocket. "I got it right here in the back of my old dollar clicker."

He opened the case, took out the picture and handed it to King. It was a little tiny thing but he could see the face plainly in the light of a street lamp as they passed.

"That's fine, Key," he said. "Sorry you had to get in a jam but glad we could get you out of it. Stop, Luga, here's the roadster."

"Holy gee," the Key exclaimed, "what are you going to do with that picture now?"

"I'm going up to Horace Mann's place, show it to the butler and see if he can recognize the face."

The Key was out of the car where they had stopped behind the roadster. He stood with the handle of the door in his hand. His mouth dropped open.

"Holy gee. How you going to get around the cops? The place is surrounded with them. They're all hiding."

"We'll have to figure that out on our way uptown," King said. "But we're not going to waste another trip on this. I'm going to see Mann's butler tonight. So long, Key. Hope you get home O.K."

CHAPTER 18
"THAT'S THE MAN!"

A SLIGHT smile spread across King's madeup face as he reached over and pulled the door out of the Key's hand, slamming it shut. The Key's mouth dropped open. Then he shook his head as they drove away and when King looked out of the rear window of the sedan he saw the Key climbing in behind the wheel of the roadster.

"Were you serious," asked the Bishop, "about going to the Mann residence?"

"Certainly," said King. "Why not?"

"But," objected the Bishop, "they've laid a trap for us there and we'll be walking right into it."

King laughed. "I doubt if the cops will do much but stand at attention when they see the Mayor and the Commissioner."

"Jolly," said the Bishop, "you're right about that. Now is the time, certainly, to go into the matter, while we're disguised as we are."

They rode on further and further uptown, reached the section in which the Horace Mann residence was located.

"Let's drive around this block once, too," said King to Luga.

"Yes, Master," said the big black.

They made one circle of the block. King was watching from one side, the Bishop from the other.

"See anything from your side, Bishop?" King asked.

"No, that is—yes, I do too. There's a figure standing across the road in the shadow of the steps there."

"And here's one standing in the shadow of this great post that forms a fence around the grounds, too," said King. "Get your vest buttoned, Bishop."

They made a turn down around the side of the block, came across the back and up the other side.

"Jolly," the Bishop groaned. "I had hoped that I wouldn't have to button this vest again."

"I don't think you will after this," King said smiling. "There's two cops talking in the shadow of that post at the back here." He glanced through the shrubbery at the house. "Not much in the line of lights on. Let's see. Seems to me the funeral is tomorrow."

"Yes," said the Bishop, "I believe it is."

"Then we're all set," said King. "It's pretty late for a call but I guess it'll do under the circumstances and considering who we are. Stop in front Luga."

"Yes, Master."

The sedan drew to the curb and stopped directly in front of the great entrance.

"They're coming," said King in a whisper to the Bishop. "I didn't know there'd be so many cops on one job. Look at them come now. They are bursting out of hallways, alleys and everything across the street."

King opened the door quickly and stepped to the sidewalk. He stood back to let the Bishop get out, heard the sound of running feet behind him, saw the swinging figures of men as they ran across the street in front of the car. Some burly fellow snatched him by the shoulder just as the Bishop was getting out, spun him around.

The false gray, close-cropped mustache that adorned his upper lip slipped from place. He bent over instantly to catch it, missed it with one hand and seemed to catch it with the other. As he did so he jerked the big cop over on top of him and they fell together on the sidewalk.

The mustache had slipped from his hand. He must find it and put it back on again. He must have that false mustache to look like the Commissioner. He heard the cop on him of him yell.

"I got him! I got him!"

Any moment now he knew that the officer's night club would crash down on his head. His hands were groping frantically on the sidewalk for that false piece of hair that had fallen from his upper lip.

Then he heard the Bishop shout in quick staccato words.

"Stop it! Stop it! What's the meaning of this! I'll have every one of you discharged."

King was still groping for his mustache when he heard a cop who was standing over him cry out.

"Holy mackerel! It's the Mayor."

"Certainly, it's the Mayor," the Bishop cried. "It's the Mayor and the Commissioner of Police, you blithering idiots. That's the Commissioner you've knocked down on the sidewalk. Are you hurt, Commissioner?"

"No," stammered King, "I don't think so." Still he hadn't found the mustache.

Then suddenly, almost miraculously, his fingers closed on it. He heard the big cop who had knocked him down apologizing profusely and trying to help him to his feet. King was struggling with the mustache on his upper lip, trying to get it back in its proper place.

He shook himself free and barked at the same time.

"Let go, you fool. Aren't you satisfied with knocking me down without dragging me all over the sidewalk?"

Then he had the mustache in place and was getting to his feet with the assistance of the Bishop. He stood there and glared from one face to another. The cops stood at rigid attention before him.

"I'd almost think," King rasped, "that this had been a plot to beat up the Mayor and myself. There must be fifteen of you around here. What is this, a cop's convention?"

A sergeant stepped up before him.

"It's all a mistake, Commissioner," he said. "Begging your pardon, sir. We've been waiting for the Secret 6 to come to talk with the butler about something he's supposed to know."

"So that's it," King rasped. "Well, it's too bad the whole police force of New York City hasn't got anything more to do than set traps for men who are doing so much good as, the Secret 6."

"But, Commissioner," ventured the sergeant. "They're making the police force look like a bunch of fools."

"Well, after some of the things I've seen pulled," the Commissioner said, "I shouldn't think that would be out of order very much." He glanced about the ring of nervous cops. "I know about fifteen policemen in this town that feel like fools right now."

"Yes, sir," said the sergeant. The others nodded meekly.

King went on. "Here the Mayor and I come to pay our respects to the body of Horace Mann and his family and what do we get but an attack by you cops who're playing a childish game. Come now; get back to your posts. You're all supposed to be patrolling some other beats in the city. We'll have no more of this foolishness."

"Yes, Commissioner," said the sergeant. He turned to the others. "Come on, you. Get goin'. Break up. Get back to your regular beats."

King nodded toward the door. "Shall we go in, Mr. Mayor?"

"By all means," said the Bishop.

AS THEY went up the stairs and the police officers broke up and left, the Bishop whispered to King.

"Let's get this over with as soon as possible. This vest is choking me."

There was a dim light burning in the hall. They rang the bell. After a considerable length of time, a butler opened the door a few inches and peered out.

"Good evening, sir," he said.

King spoke up. "The Mayor and Commissioner of Police have come to pay their respects to the body of Horace Mann," he said. "We are grieved that we can't attend the funeral tomorrow but business calls us out of town and the only time we could spare was this late hour of the night."

The butler's eyes widened and so did the door opening.

"Yes, sir," he said. "Come in, your Honor and you Commissioner. I'll show you to the parlor where the master's body is lying in state."

They followed him in and he closed the door. He led them to the great parlor which was draped in black. At the far end a casket stood on a pedestal.

"There he is, sir," he said.

"Thank you," said the Bishop. King nodded and they walked over and looked at the body of a man they had never seen before.

That must be Horace Mann. The head was turned on the right side as it lay in the casket. That was so the bullet hole in the side of the head wouldn't show. They looked reverently on the stilled form for a moment. Then King turned to the butler.

"As I recall," he said, "one of my men reported seeing a large man well over six feet tall leave the place perhaps an hour before the body of Mr. Mann was found. You admitted him, didn't you?"

The butler bowed. "Yes, sir."

"Would you know that man if you saw him again?" King asked.

The butler nodded. "I believe so."

King took the tiny picture of Henry Gilson from his pocket.

"That's a picture that was taken almost ten years ago," he said, "but is that the man? Do you recognize a likeness?"

The butler studied the picture for a moment and then he nodded.

"Yes, sir," he said. "I can see a strong resemblance. That's the same face, sir. I'd swear to it."

King put the picture back in his pocket. "Good, and thank you. I think we may go, Mr. Mayor."

"Yes," the Bishop half groaned. "By all means."

The butler ushered them out of the house and closed the front door behind them. They went down the steps and into the rear seat of the car without saying a word. There was not a cop in sight.

The Bishop dropped into the seat, unbuttoned his vest hurriedly and took a long breath as the car moved away.

"Jolly," he said. "That's a relief."

"Now we head for home, Luga," King said.

"Well," King said as they rolled on, "I think that just about clinches the whole thing. One thing sure it presents itself in the form of four or five giants now which may on the other hand develop into only one giant after all."

"One giant," demanded the Bishop. "How on earth did you figure that out?"

King switched on the dome light of the car and handed him the tiny picture of Henry Gilson.

"Take a good look at that," he said. "There's something familiar about it, isn't there?"

The Bishop leaned forward and studied it.

"Yes," he said. "There is but I can't seem to place it."

"You were there at Pennington's tonight when the giant came."

"Certainly. I'll never forget that as long as I live."

"Well," said King. "Think of the face that the giant had and take a good look at that picture."

202

"Why," said the Bishop, "I don't see just what you mean."

"Just think it over," said King. "Maybe you will. I'll explain a little more fully when we get back to the cabin. If the Doctor is there perhaps he can throw more light on it. I think the Key has accomplished more tonight in stealing this from the District Attorney's office than he expected when he first thought of it as a good joke on the D.A."

They were crossing the bridge into Brooklyn. They drove on and turned on the north shore road. King leaned forward to Luga.

"Take a swing up around through Glen Cove. I think I'll have to alter my plans a little with Mr. Pennington."

They swung up toward Glen Cove and Luga, with an unfaltering sense of direction, found the Pennington place in the early hours of the morning. Turning into that eventful drive, he drew up before the door.

King got out. It took several minutes to arouse anyone in the household. Then Mr. Pennington himself, answered the door garbed in his dressing gown. He peered out at King through the crack in the door.

"Good heavens, Commissioner," he said, "that is, you are the Commissioner, aren't you?"

King stared at him a split second and then remembered and laughed.

"I had almost forgotten," he said, "that I was still disguised as the Police Commissioner. I'm King. Sorry to disappoint you."

"That certainly is no disappointment, King," said Pennington. "Come in, won't you? What has been going on?"

"WE HAD a little work to do down at police headquarters," King said as he stepped inside. "One of the Secret 6 was under arrest down there and we had to get him out. I'm sorry to awaken you at this hour but I have changed my plans regarding going to Chicago. Has anything happened since I've been gone?"

"Nothing except that I've gotten in touch with Doctor Rhinehart. And you didn't disturb my rest. I've been lying awake all night since you left waiting for the giant to come back."

"What did Doctor Rhinehart say?" King asked.

"I told him the situation and he didn't seem to know exactly what I was talking about. He said he was needed at the hospital and didn't want to leave unless it was absolutely necessary."

"I stopped," King said, "to tell you that I've changed the hour of reaching Chicago tomorrow. Instead of three o'clock, I think I can make it by noon. That'll get us back here a little before dark. Would you mind if I call the doctor myself?"

"I'd be more than glad to have you," Pennington said. "Perhaps you can convince him that he should come."

King put through a call for Doctor F. C. Rhinehart at the Hospital for the Aged in Chicago. There was a long wait, and then a deliberate kindly voice came back to him over the earphone.

"This is Doctor Rhinehart," he said.

"Doctor Rhinehart," King said. "I'm calling you on the same subject that Mr. Pennington called you about a little earlier tonight. Did he tell you about the giant wanting you to come prepared to operate?"

There was a hesitation at the other end of the line.

"It does seem as though he said something about coming to operate. Yes, I believe he mentioned something about a giant, too. I haven't the slightest idea what—"

"You would have had a very definite idea," King said, "if you had been here earlier tonight and seen the giant. I'm going to fly out to Chicago to get you. I'll be there tomorrow at noon. You'll come or I'll report it to the police."

The doctor hesitated. "I shouldn't come," he said. "I have some very important research work to do here. I can't really understand anything that you are telling me."

"Listen," King said. "Have you ever heard of the Secret 6?"

"Good heavens, yes," said the doctor. "Who hasn't? But what—" his voice was shaky now.

"Plenty," King snapped, "I was the one who talked to you the night you were out calling your giant dogs. I think knowing that will make your work in Chicago seem very unimportant!"

"I—I'll be waiting at the airport for you," Rhinehart stammered.

"Very well," said King. "I'll meet you there at twelve noon tomorrow, Chicago time. Look for a low-winged six-passenger monoplane painted a blood-red all over."

He hung up the receiver.

"I think," he said rising and turning to Pennington, "that fixes that. Now we've got something definite to tell the giant if he comes back."

"Yes. Why—yes," said Pennington, nervously. "That'll be some consolation. I wish to heaven that I could believe he would never come back."

"I'm afraid he will," said King, "so you might as well be prepared. Goodnight, Mr. Pennington."

He went out and climbed into the back seat of the sedan.

"Now we go home, Luga," he said.

The car sped out on the main highway and rolled on.

They found the other members of the Secret 6 waiting for them when they reached the cabin. Shakespeare was asleep and snoring laboriously.

"What news?" asked the Doctor and the Key almost in the same breath.

King took a cloth and began wiping the makeup off his face. Then he handed it to the Bishop who did the same.

"How the deuce did you get out of that trap the cops had at Horace Mann's joint?" the Key asked.

"I almost didn't," King grinned, "but I guess those cops are scared enough so that they won't jump on anyone again before they look twice. We went up as the Mayor and the Police Commissioner."

He reached in his pocket and took out the tiny round photograph of Henry Gilson that the Key had cut from the group picture.

"I'd like to have you all take a good look at that. Everybody that is, except you, Key. You didn't see the giant at Pennington's tonight."

"Holy gee," said the Key. "Did you? How big was he?"

"I don't know," said King. "We guessed that he must have been between fifteen and twenty feet tall," he said casually, watching the expression on the Key's face.

"Huh," exploded the Key and his mouth dropped open.

The rest were looking at the photograph.

"By George," exploded the Doctor, "that face looks very much like the face of the giant."

"That's what I thought," said King.

"Now that you mentioned it," said the Bishop, "there is indeed a striking resemblance there."

"I thought you'd hit after a while," King said.

"But who under the sun is this," the Doctor demanded. "Is this Henry Gilson's picture that the Key stole from the District Attorney's office?"

"I'll say it is," laughed the Key. "And what a joke it's going to be on the D.A. when he finds out that's cut out of the group. Boy, if the cops think they had a reason to kid him last night they'll sure have a chance to laugh their heads off when they find out tomorrow."

"That'll be counteracted," King smiled, "when they find out that the Mayor and the Commissioner weren't there at headquarters to take you out. There won't be so much of a laugh about that."

"But I don't understand," said the Bishop. "How do you connect the fact that this picture of Henry Gilson looks like the giant who came into Mr. Pennington's home last evening?"

"I'll answer that with another question," said King. "How do you connect the fact that Horace Mann's butler tonight identified this picture of Henry Gilson, who stands five feet six inches or less, with the man well over six feet in height who called to see Horace Mann?"

"Is that a fact," cried the Doctor.

"Absolutely," said King. "We have three identifications now. The butler has identified this picture as the man over six feet tall who came to Mann's house that night. Mark Fiddler admitted that the giant who was about seven feet tall and beat him up was Henry Gilson. Now we, ourselves, identified this photograph as the giant who stands somewhere between fifteen and twenty feet tall, who smashed in the side of Pennington's house a few hours ago."

The others of the Secret 6 stared about them, all except Shakespeare who continued to snore. King's eyes were on the Doctor.

"Doctor," he said. "You stated a short time ago that the name of Doctor F. C. Rhinehart sounded familiar to you. Have you any recollection where you heard or read that name before? Can't you think where it was? Could it have been some article that Rhinehart wrote in a medical magazine or some other phase of medicine?"

The Doctor's eyes narrowed and he stared into space for a moment, deep in thought.

"By George," he said. "I've got it. Yes, I know where it was that I read that and what it was about. Good heavens, I never thought about it."

CHAPTER 19
THE MAN MONSTER

"YOU'RE RIGHT, King," the Doctor went on. "I had read that name, Doctor Rhinehart in a medical magazine and I remember the article now. It had to do with a new type of gland operation. He had experimented on animals and said it worked quite satisfactorily. To some extent it blasted the theory that the pituitary gland controlled the growth of the body, made some people large and some people small as the gland reacted. He claimed that he had found another inner gland, a far smaller body in the same socket beneath the pituitary gland. A gland that was really part of the string that attached the pituitary gland to the rest of the body, that was in reality the gland that controlled the growth.

"He claimed that he had operated on some larger animals with the result that in one case he had made a dog grow to almost twice its normal size. In some way he stimulates the activity of this gland which he has discovered and called the pituitary gland."

King stared at the Doctor.

"By George, that's the answer," he cried. "Rhinehart operated on those dogs and made them huge, and then he tried it on human beings."

"It would certainly seem so," said the Doctor. "Yet to a practical medical man the idea seems too outrageously fantastic to believe. If it's true, it answers the question. It would solve the mystery of the several giants.

"Hey," said the Key, "suppose you guys talk plain English for a while so I can understand you. What do you mean about this solving the mystery of the several giants?"

King smiled. "Well, maybe this will bring it out a little clearer," he said. "We've forgotten to tell you what went on at Pennington's house. The giant called him up yesterday afternoon and wanted him to get in touch with a Doctor F.C. Rhinehart and have him come out at once prepared to operate. We tried to get this doctor and found he was in Chicago for a few days. I told the giant our Doctor would do his best if he explained his trouble. But he said no, he couldn't help him any. We've been trying to figure out just why the giant must have this particular Doctor Rhinehart and now the Doctor has solved it. Apparently Doctor Rhinehart has operated on Henry Gilson and ever since Gilson has been growing because of the superior action of the new gland that the doctor discovered."

"Holy gee!" exploded the Key. "This guy ain't never goin' to stop growing?"

"That's the question," the Doctor said, "that can't be answered until we see how this experiment works out."

"And in the meantime," King said, "we've got a monster wandering around this part of the country." He turned to the Doctor. "I doubt very much Doctor, if even machinegun bullets would have very much effect on that monster man. If we're right about our guess as to his growth, there's no telling how much he has grown since we saw him several hours ago. It's the most ghastly unbelievable thing I've ever heard of."

"Holy gee, then all these guys we thought was different guys is just one guy growin' up."

"Yes," said King, "that's the only logical explanation as far as I can see. Let's trace it back now and see how it lines up. The first time we hear of this giant is when he's a little over six feet tall, and is seen coming out of the house of Horace Mann.

"The next time we find him, Flo sees him leaving Mark Fiddler's apartment with something under his arm that Fiddler admits are the stolen records. Fiddler has been badly beaten up and is unconscious. He swears that the man is almost seven feet tall. That means that he has grown eight or ten inches in a short time. Apparently he's growing faster and faster as times goes on. Something, perhaps, like the square of numbers increases. Two times two is four, three times three is nine, and four times four is sixteen and so on. The bigger he gets, the faster he grows.

"The next place we find him is at Pennington's house. It seems Mark Fiddler or his men have left a blackmail note there and they've also left a big shoe print in the soft earth of the flower garden in front of the house. Only the shoe was false—made of a couple of boards nailed together. The giant was plenty big then. As we saw him he was hunched over. What little we could see of him in the dark but even at that he was eight or ten feet tall.

"Then he appears again. We trailed him from Pennington's the first time and we found footprints thirty-five inches long and forty-one inches long and the last one stretches to forty-two inches long a short time afterwards. We assumed there had been two giants that had met at the quarry but if we're on the right mental track now, the thirty-five inch footprints that we found were made before he went into the mine to take a nap.

"He grew while he was resting and when he came out his foot-print was forty-one inches long and an hour or two later his foot-print was forty-two inches long.

"Then he appears at Pennington's place a few hours ago and he's grown to be a man fifteen or *twenty* feet high and built in proportion. He's grown so big that the large pants which he wore before are only big enough for a loin cloth now. Each time we saw a larger track or a larger man we thought it was a different giant."

"To be sure," said the Bishop. "And why shouldn't we?"

"Yes," said the Doctor. "I was beginning to believe there was a whole organization of giants."

"I think," said King, "we'll find out before we get through that it is one giant continually growing bigger."

The Doctor shook his head. "It's the weirdest thing I ever heard of in my life."

King smiled as he glanced at him. "Perhaps you don't believe it, Doctor."

"I can't help believing anything that I've seen with my own eyes. It's the most ghastly thing I've ever heard of in my life."

"You really believe it's possible?" the Bishop asked. The Doctor shook his head.

"No man has any right to say that anything isn't possible. Some very strange things have happened in the medical profession. Things that when they're explained afterwards are quite simple but when they happen to someone who doesn't understand, they certainly appear to border on the miraculous."

King got up and stretched.

"If it's all the same to you gentlemen," he said, "I think I'm going to turn in. Unless I'm badly mistaken we're in for a very large day tomorrow. Goodnight."

KING WAS tired and he slept. He woke up at the first break of dawn, the first one to stir. With the slight sound that he made while dressing, Luga was up and hurriedly preparing breakfast.

"Luga go with you?" the big black asked.

"No, Big Boy," King said, "not this time. I want to go light so I can make the trip in as much of a hurry as possible. I think you'll do more good here. Stick to the rest of the band and protect them, won't you."

"Yes, Master," the big black said. "Certainly."

King ate hurriedly. When he was finished he pushed back his plate and got up. The rest were still asleep.

"Say goodbye to them, Luga, and tell them I'll try to be back before sundown if possible," King said.

Then he was gone, striding toward the long narrow airport that was hidden in the woods back of the cabin. He climbed into the pilot's seat, started the motor and let it warm. He tested the controls. Then when everything was ready he gave her the gun and the great ship rumbled down the field and zoomed into the air.

He turned west, reached up over his head and pulled the lever that let the exhaust escape before it reached the great muffler. The giant engine bellowed out in the clear morning.

At three thousand feet Manhattan with a dull haze about it, loomed in the distance. Then he was thundering over it heading for the rugged country of Pennsylvania, the aviator's graveyard. He flew higher now, watching his compass and other instruments. He had better than a half tank of gas. That would get him as far as Cleveland. There he could gas up and go on.

Somehow things seemed fairly settled for the time being. He was satisfied that they had solved at least part of the mystery. Perhaps the doctor would enlighten them on the rest.

The big motor kept on with a reassuring bellow of sound. Then the little red light on his dash began winking at him. That was attached to the two-way, dot, dash radio system that the Doctor had installed in the plane some time before.

When the red light winked, it meant that they were trying to reach him with a message. King threw a switch and clamped a pair of ear-phones on his head. Da—de—de—da—de—de. A message began coming over and King spelled it out as it came.

GOOD MORNING. WHAT'S THE IDEA OF SNEAK-ING OUT ON US WITHOUT WAKING US UP? HOW IS EVERYTHING

SECRET 6.

King threw the switch in reverse and began tapping out an answer in reply.

JUST PASSED BELLEFONTE BEACON. EVERY-THING O.K. WHAT'S THE NEWS FROM YOUR END?

He threw the switch and the reply came back.

SITTING DOWN TO BREAKFAST. WISH WE WERE WITH YOU. GOOD LUCK.

THE DOCTOR.

King grinned as he threw off the switch and took off the headphones.

"Great gang," he said, "we ought to be able to accomplish anything with that bunch."

He thundered on. The country flattened out as he neared Cleveland, farms and fields became more in evidence. He struck the south shore of Lake Erie. Very soon now he knew he would see, from his five-thousand foot altitude, the city of Cleveland spread out like a giant nest of doll houses, ahead, and as that thought came to him he saw the city far in the distance.

He turned and skirted the city and looked for the airport on the other side. It was very easy to find. Then he slowed his throttle and came down for a landing.

Ten minutes to gas up. Then he was in the plane and on the way again droning on toward Chicago.

Then across the flatter country. He cut across the southern end of Lake Michigan and from there found the airport on the side of the great city of Chicago.

He had made good time coming out. He had just time enough to gas up and buy some sandwiches.

He cut the gun and glided down to land. He left the ship to be serviced and walked over to the restaurant. He ordered sandwiches and a couple of bottles of milk for the return trip. He watched them fill the tanks, and checked the motor himself, now that it was cool and all the time he was watching for the doctor to drive up.

Minutes passed. He started the motor so that it would be warm when Doctor Rhinehart arrived. More minutes passed. It was after twelve. King watched anxiously now. Was the doctor going back on his word? He considered taking a cab and driving to the Hospital for the Aged to learn what was holding him up. Then he heard a siren and stared down the road.

A long gray car was clipping off the mileage as it tore for the field. It swerved in the gate and stopped near the administration building.

Then a small nervous little man leaped out of the front seat.

King left his plane and strode rapidly out across the tarmac. The nervous little man was staring at the plane and walking toward him now. King smiled.

"You are Doctor Rhinehart," he asked.

The doctor nodded. "Yes," he said suddenly quite calm. "You're—"

"Never mind that here," King said. "Let's go."

"About lunch, do you plan to stop on the way or—" asked the doctor.

"I have some sandwiches and milk in the cabin," King said.

"Excellent," said the doctor, climbing in.

King pointed him to the right hand seat in front. He took the one opposite.

"Just keep your hands and feet off the dual controls, Doctor," he said, "and we'll get along nicely."

216

HE REACHED up and flipped the muffler on again so that the lessening of the noise would permit them to talk more easily.

"I hope," the doctor said, "you will believe me when I tell you that all this is accidental on my part. That is, I didn't plan these dogs or the man as a menace to society."

"Well, you certainly messed up things properly whether you meant to or not."

Doctor Rhinehart looked at him gravely; changed the subject. "You say your name is—"

"King," was the reply.

"Oh, yes," said the doctor. "King, that's right. Well, King, I'll tell you what I know and it will be the truth. Believe me, I'm not a fiend. I'm a medical man. To be exact, I'm a gland specialist. You say it was three or four nights ago that a man well over six feet was seen coming out of Horace Mann's place an hour or so before Mann committed suicide?"

King nodded.

"That, I think," said the doctor, "ties up with what happened to me. It was about two weeks ago that I advertised for a patient. Now that sounds strange, doesn't it? You see, I have been experimenting with this pituitary gland with animals with quite a degree of success. As a matter of fact, I felt there was no danger because none of the animals I had operated upon, died.

"So I advertised for some small person who wished to be made larger. I got an almost immediate reply from a small man who said his name was Wilson."

King took the picture of Henry Gilson out of his pocket and handed it to the doctor.

"Is that the man," he asked.

"Why, why, yes," said the doctor. "Yes, that's the very man."

"That's Henry Gilson," said King. "Not Wilson—Gilson."

"Why," said the doctor, "I'm almost positive that I understood him correctly."

"No doubt you did," said King. "He probably told you that his name was Wilson.

"Go on with your story, doctor."

"Well, this man Wilson, or Gilson, came to me almost three weeks ago and offered to let me operate on him. He was five feet five-and-a-half inches tall. I measured him very carefully because that was part of my experiment. I asked him particularly why he wanted the operation because he appeared to me to be a man of considerable intelligence.

"He said a man much larger than himself had insulted him the night before—had as a matter of fact, beat him up a bit. He wanted to grow larger so he could go back and beat up his enemy.

"He remained in my private sanitarium, which is part of my house, several days under careful watch. During that time he began to grow. The last report showed he had gained about an inch a day and he was beginning to grow considerably faster toward the last. Then one night when he was over six feet tall and I was overjoyed at the results of my operation, he escaped. I had some dogs that had grown huge. He let those out too. I was calling them when you first saw me."

King tensed as the red light in the instrument board began to flicker back and forth. A message was coming through from the Secret 6 now. He put on the headphones and flipped on the switch.

CHAPTER 20
THE GIANT'S SWEETHEART

AT THE other end of the wireless the Doctor was ticking away frantically. The message read:

JUST GOT WORD FROM THE DUMMY THAT THE POLICE HAVE BEEN ADVISED OF A GIANT GONE WILD IN LONG ISLAND. HE'S AT LEAST THIRTY FEET TALL. SOME REPORTS SAY FORTY FEET. HE'S ON A WILD RAMPAGE. HE'S SMASHING DOWN HOUSES AND DESTROYING PROPERTY IN GENERAL. SEVERAL FARMERS HAVE COMPLAINED ABOUT THEIR LIVESTOCK VANISHING AND FINDING FOOTPRINTS SIX FEET LONG IN SOFT EARTH. SEVERAL PEOPLE REPORT HAVING SEEN HIM. HE'S CRUSHED SEVERAL WHO TRIED TO STOP HIM. THE POLICE ARE MASSING FORCES TO RUN HIM DOWN AND KILL HIM. HURRY BACK AS FAST AS YOU CAN.
SECRET 6.

"I wonder if King will catch that message. Personally I'm stumped to know what to do."

The Key nodded but he didn't grin.

"King asked this morning for any news as it came," he said. "He's sure got an earful now."

The Doctor was slipping the earphones on his head, listening tensely. He heard the da—de—da—de—da of the answer from King.

I'M ALMOST AS FAR AS CLEVELAND WITH THE DOCTOR. THINK I HAVE ENOUGH GAS TO GET THROUGH. WON'T TAKE THE TIME TO STOP. COMING WIDE OPEN.

KING.

The Doctor took the 'phones off his ears. "He'll be here as soon as he can," he said.

"Well, what do we do now," asked the Key.

A humming sound came from the shortwave radio receiver.

"Wait a minute," said the Doctor. "There's somebody else."

Silence fell in the cabin. Then the voice of Flo came drifting easily through the speaker of the shortwave set.

"What's this I hear about a giant running loose all over Long Island? Everybody is talking about it. Are any of you in danger? Is King in danger? Is this the same case we have been on?" And right there another voice cut in on her conversation. Flo was just saying, "If you can hear me try to get to a 'phone and let me know where I can see the giant," when they heard a voice coming hurriedly, tangling with hers.

"Hello, hello, hello, Secret 6. This is Legs Larkin. My daughter at Pennington's house called. Pennington thinks the giant is on his way there. He's been moving across country by the side of the main highway on the north shore. He's got to be almost fifty feet high. He is on his way toward Pennington's. He's destroying everything in his path. Pennington wants me to tell you to hurry before everybody is killed. This is Legs Larkin."

The radio fell silent. Men stared at each other.

"Jolly," said the Bishop, "I wish I could think of something to do. There seems to be no stopping this giant."

"I'm afraid not," said the Doctor. "Not if he's grown to be forty or fifty feet tall."

"It seems as though we ought to do something," Shakespeare said.

"Yes," said the Doctor, "if we don't do anything more than try to get to the giant and quiet him down until the doctor comes."

A whistling sound came from the speaker of the short-wave set again. They tensed to listen again and heard Flo's voice once more through the air to them.

"I've gotten hold of Legs Larkin on the 'phone. I've been trying all the gang. Legs tells me that the giant is on his way to Pennington's house. I'm not going to let you fellows have all the fun. Tell King I'm going out to Pennington's."

"No," yelled the Key, as though Flo the Fleecer could hear him. "Don't come out, Flo. You're liable to get killed like the rest of them." Then suddenly the Key realized that Flo couldn't hear him.

"Come on," he said. "We've got to get to a 'phone and call Flo. We've got to stop her."

"We may as well all go," said the Bishop.

"Just a moment," said the Doctor, "until I gather up my sending and receiving set."

He was gathering up his radio equipment to be installed in the car. Then suddenly the Dummy's voice sounded in a dull monotone from the speaker.

"Just heard something else around police headquarters. The cops say that the Secret 6 and the giant are all teamed up together."

The Doctor shook his head. "That certainly is a new one," he said. "I never dreamed that the police would flatter me to that extent."

The Dummy had stopped talking. They left the cabin hurriedly now. Luga helped him carry the two-way radio set that would keep them in touch with King's plane. Quickly the Doctor installed it against the back of the front seat of the sedan, turned it on and listened.

"There," he said, "it's working O.K. Luga, you might as well drive and stop at the first place that has a telephone."

THE BIG black slid in behind the wheel. The Bishop was beside him. The other three climbed into the back seat. The Doctor was playing with his radio set.

"Wait, I've got something," he said. "It's a message from King. He's explaining Doctor Rhinehart's point of view."

Luga was rolling out the bedrock drive and turning east on the main highway.

"Shall I go slow?" he asked. "So you can hear better, Doctor?"

"No. I can hear all right. Step on it."

The car rolled to a higher speed.

"It's just as we thought," the Doctor said. "Doctor Rhinehart is the gland specialist that I mentioned. He says about three weeks ago Henry Gilson came to him in answer to an ad of his and wanted to be a bigger man. The doctor operated and after Gilson had gained a few inches he escaped from the sanatorium. Something about a larger man that he wanted to beat up."

"Holy Gee," said the Key. "That must have been Mark Fiddler."

"Exactly," said the Doctor. "King says they've passed Cleveland, now. That's the end of the message. Wait, I'll answer him."

He worked a key on top of the set. The Doctor was telling King what was happening at their end. He finished his answer, took the earphones off his head for a moment and mopped his brow.

"There," he said, "that ought to give him something to think about."

They swung through a small town. Luga brought the car to a stop in front of the only drug store there. The Key leaped out of the car and ran in. A woman was sitting in the drug store sobbing. The druggist was giving her first aid treatment. As the Key passed to the telephone booth he heard the woman sob brokenly.

"He killed my husband and smashed our house."

The druggist was trying to comfort her as he worked.

"There, there," he said, "the giant's gone on. He won't come back here."

The Key pushed into the telephone booth, got some change ready and called Flo's apartment.

"I'm sorry," the operator said, "No one answers there."

"Why, for cryin' out loud, try 'em again," the Key choked.

Then suddenly the wires went dead. He jiggled the hook frantically. But it was hopeless. He came out of the booth. The woman was still talking, sometimes in shrieks, sometimes only with gasping sobs.

"My husband found him in our pasture. He was higher than any of the trees on our farm. He was eating our cattle. Eating whole cows like they were so many pork chops. Then my husband got his gun and went out hoping he could drive him away. And he's got a good gun.

"He shot again and again at that giant but he must have a hide like iron because the shots simply bounced away. Then he said something to my husband. It was so loud that it sounded like thunder. I couldn't understand a word he said. My husband emptied the rest of the bullets in his rifle at him. Then he ran.

"The giant took a long stride and then another and—" her voice rose to a high pitched scream—"he stepped on him. Do you hear me? Stepped on my husband with one of those huge feet."

That was plenty for the Key. He rushed out to the car. The roads were jammed with traffic now, but all the cars were going the other way, driving like mad.

The sedan of the Secret 6 was the only one traveling toward the giant.

Suddenly the Bishop, who was in front with Luga, pointed far away down the road. There a giant form loomed far above the tree tops.

A small village lay in its path. Far down the road they could see men out in the street and hiding behind bushes and houses.

The giant swerved suddenly. His great foot swung through the air in a gigantic arc and in the one kick he sent half a dozen houses sprawling and flattened them out on the ground.

The men sitting in that sedan as they rode along could almost see the giant grow as they watched him. He flattened the entire village and pushed on. They saw the giant stop in a pasture.

At least twenty-five cows stampeded to the other end and broke through a pasture fence that normally no cattle would tackle.

The giant turned his head, looked down and saw them. He bent down and made a wild lunge with his hand. With two monstrous strokes, he flattened the cattle.

Then he squatted down on his haunches, picked them up one by one and thrust them in his huge mouth. Suddenly the Doctor bellowed:

"We've got to stop this some way. Luga there's a road across the field where the giant is eating those cattle. Drive over there as fast as you can. I'm going to talk to him."

The Key stared at him.

"Holy Gee. Have you gone crazy, Doc?"

"Drive over there," boomed the Doctor again. "We've got to stop this thing somehow. I'm going to get on the running board and tell the giant, if he can hear anything, that King is on his way back with Doctor Rhinehart."

The giant turned his head angrily as they came near.

THE DOCTOR was on the running board now. He was holding out his hand in a token of friendship.

"Doctor Rhinehart is on his way by airplane, giant," he called out.

"That's good," he said. "Hope he isn't too late. How soon will he get here?"

"Wait! I'll find out," said the Doctor. "I've got a wireless set right here in the car."

"Alright," he thundered, "I'll wait. Send your message."

The men sat petrified in the car. The Doctor had all he could do to keep his hand steady as he sent that message asking King how long it would be, told him what had happened and begged him to hurry for the love of humanity. Then they listened. Listened more tensely than he had ever listened to a radio set before and the message began coming back to him from King.

WE HAVE PASSED BELLEFONTE AND WE'RE COMING JUST AS FAST AS WE CAN. OUGHT NOT TO BE QUITE AN HOUR.

"What did he say," roared the giant in what was to him a whisper.

"He says it ought not to be quite an hour before he gets here."

"Thank heaven," the giant's voice boomed. "Tell him to land at Pennington's estate."

"Very well," said the Doctor.

Then suddenly as he began work on the wireless key, the giant turned and stood on his feet. His enormous hand came down over the top of the car. He clutched the car between his great

fingers, lifted it and started off at a great stride. The Doctor's
fingers were shaking as he sent his next message to King.

THE GIANT IS CARRYING THE FIVE OF US,
CAR AND ALL, IN ONE HAND LIKE A TOY. HE
WANTS ME TO GIVE YOU ORDERS TO LAND AT
THE PENNINGTON ESTATE. FOR THE LOVE OF
HEAVEN, HURRY. IF YOU FAIL WE'LL ALL BE DEAD
MEN.

"Did you send the message?" asked the giant.

"Yes," said the Doctor.

"What does he say?"

"He's answering now. Wait," the Doctor said. "Yes. He says it
will be all right. He'll try to land there."

"Good," said the giant.

Suddenly there was a staccato sound from the edge of the road
they were skirting. *Tac, tac, tac.* It was the stutter of machinegun
fire. Looking down with horror from the car windows forty or
fifty feet above the ground, they could see men in the uniforms
of state police cutting loose at the giant with Tommy guns.

They heard the giant's voice roar.

"You think you're doing me harm with those machine guns
but you're only tickling me and hardly that. If you fire again I'll
sweep you all into grease spots!"

The firing ceased. The troopers ran from ambush and leaped
into their cars.

After a moment the giant said as softly as he could, "I suppose you think I should laugh at the way they ran from me. There's nothing funny about my predicament. I hope you realize that."

Far ahead the Pennington estate was now visible. The giant was heading for it, walking with great strides through the tree-lined streets of the village.

He came to a fine church, a frame structure with a pointed steeple at the front. He stopped a moment in his long strides and stared at it. He was just about as tall as the steeple.

"I'll need a place to stay out of the weather while I'm recuperating from the operation," he bellowed in that voice of his. "This church should serve."

With his foot he kicked in the front of the church. Then, still holding the car quite close to him, he crawled inside the edifice. With a gigantic heave he tore the building, sides and all, loose from the floor. He stood up now. Then he walked off toward the estate of Pennington with the church hanging about his head and shoulders and the sedan with five of the Secret 6 in his hand hanging down by his side.

They reached the Pennington estate. There wasn't room for him to pass between two trees so he pushed them aside, broke them like match sticks.

He reached a wide space in the lawn, stooped and settled down with the church on his shoulders. In that position he stood up the church as a child would set up a toy house. Then he crawled out from the interior.

He set the car and the five men in it very gently upon the lawn.

"There," he said, "you'll stay there until the doctor arrives."

Heads bobbed inside the car. No one could speak. Luga climbed out of the car from the driver's seat. He looked like a tiny black doll in front of the huge giant.

The Doctor was working with the radio.

"For the love of heaven, hurry with that doctor," his message to King said.

Suddenly a cry sounded from the entrance of the estate. A young woman came toward the car of the Secret 6.

"King! King!" she called.

It was Flo. Her face was white but her cheeks were flushed. She looked particularly attractive on this late afternoon, in a dark serge suit that fitted her snugly.

"Wh—where's King," she exclaimed.

The Key found his voice.

"Get out of here," he yelled, "before something happens to you. King's gone with the plane. He's bringing back a doctor from Chicago."

"But, but," the girl choked, "he'll be killed. The giant will—"

The Key rushed at her, pleading.

"Beat it, kid," he yelled, "before it's too late."

Then suddenly a rumbling sound came from the giant. All eyes turned in horror to see him looking down. He was gazing down at Flo and a hungry, greedy look had come over his face. Flo turned with a scream but the giant was too quick for her and his arm was too long.

He reached out and grasped her. She screamed and fought back. The Key was trying to fight off that hand but it was like a rabbit trying to attack an elephant. The giant lifted Flo from the ground and raised her up and up.

CHAPTER 21
DYNAMITE WINGS

HE HELD the screaming, fighting girl up before his face, that face that was far longer than the girl's entire body. "You're a beauty," he roared. "Aren't you? If I had someone as beautiful as you, well, nearly as large as I am, to be my queen, I'd be tempted to try for the job of ruler of the world."

Somehow Flo got control of her wits.

"If you think you can win the love of a woman by brute force, you're badly mistaken, giant." There was a quaver in her voice that she was trying to hide. She was fighting bravely to keep calm. "You know the Stone Age passed away long ago."

The giant laughed. It was obvious that he was trying to laugh softly but it came in a cackling bellow.

"There might be other ways," he said. "Suppose I made you a giant like I am. Suppose," he went on, "there were just two of us on earth, of my size. I think you would come to love me before we got through."

He turned and tore off a side of the belfry in the church. Then he placed the girl gently through the opening.

"There," he said, "you can stay there until the doctor comes, and we'll see—"

He stopped short, stared toward the west again.

"Just in time," he roared. "The plane is coming. It's a red plane. Is that the one?"

"Yes," said the Doctor, "that's the plane with Doctor Rhinehart."

The plane came on at top speed. It circled the Pennington estate. They could see King staring in astonishment through the pilot's window of the cabin. He circled again and then came down. He climbed out of the cabin with the doctor.

"You've come just in time," the giant roared. "I was going to have you perform another operation on me in the hope that it might make me smaller or at least stop my growth, but I think I've now reached my maximum and I've changed my mind. I've decided to rule the world and in the belfry is a beautiful young woman. You'll perform the same operation upon her that you performed on me. She will grow to be a fitting size to be my queen. Together she and I will rule the world. Your weapons cannot harm me. I'm too big."

The little doctor glanced at him defiantly.

"You're mad, giant. You're insane."

"Yes," roared the giant, "and you made me this way. Now it's too late to do anything for me. You can make this girl so she will grow so that I may have a partner in this monstrous life."

"I won't do it," shouted the doctor.

"No!" bellowed the giant. "Then I'll kill you." He swung his great arm, picked up the doctor, case and all, and set him in the belfry.

"I'll give you an hour. If the operation isn't performed within an hour, I'll kill you both."

King had stood like a frozen statue while all this had been going on. Now while the giant's interest was concentrated on the belfry where he had placed the doctor together with Flo, he slipped around the corner of the partly demolished church and under cover of that he ran toward his plane that was still idling.

There was a wild roar as the plane took the air. The giant turned at the sound of the motor.

"Stop! Stop!" he bellowed.

Then he reached out his free hand and rushed forward to grasp the plane. He just barely missed catching the tail as the plane took to the air.

Luga, the great black Zulu chief, was staring up at the trees that bordered the side of the church. They were strange trees from another land. Trees that had long vine-like branches hanging from them. Trees from another continent. He started to move away but the Doctor caught his arm.

"Where are you going, Luga?" he asked in a whisper.

"Luga go to belfry in church. Get girl. Luga get Flo."

"Go to it, boy," he said, "and good luck. We'll try to keep the giant's attention down here on the ground."

It was growing dusk. Luga moved like a black panther from tree to tree. He reached the one nearest the church. They saw him disappear behind the trunk. The Bishop called out to the giant now.

"Giant," he said, "Do you realize what you're doing. You're growing mad!"

The giant glared down at him.

"I think I know what I'm doing," he boomed. "I certainly hope so."

"One man can't possibly conquer the world. Undoubtedly you're the biggest man that's ever lived but on the other hand, there are inventions that man can make that can kill you."

THE GIANT mouth dropped open for a moment. In that instant they saw Luga swing from one of the long limbs of the tree next to the church. They saw him swing to the ledge behind the steeple. Then he dropped there and they couldn't see him.

The giant couldn't see him either for the steeple hid him from view.

Then the whine of an airplane came from the southwest. The giant seemed to stiffen. The men on the ground thought that the monstrous face turned a little whiter shade.

"I'll take my chances," he said rather desperately.

The airplane came tearing down now, machine guns stuttering wildly. They were aiming at the face of the giant, but the giant simply threw up his free arm for a moment to protect his eyes and face. His eyes peered over the top of that arm.

At the same instant the branch of the tree that Luga held, moved. The giant reached suddenly as the plane dived. His left hand shot upward. It grasped the plane in midair, carried along by it like the hand of a ball player moves with a fast thrown ball.

Then Luga was swinging from the top of the church roof. Swinging, holding the branch in one hand and the girl in his other arm. The giant turned just in time to see them swinging down in a broad arc. The hand that had covered the opening to the church belfry contracted instantly. The steeple toppled over

He grasped the plane in mid-air.

like match wood as he crushed the belfry and Doctor Rhinehart inside of it.

He leaped to catch the great Zulu chief and the girl as they swung on the long tree branch away from the church. He missed. In a fit of powerful rage he hurled the wreckage of the police plane, pilot, engine, machine guns and all, at Luga and Flo.

He missed again by a scant foot or two. They swung up under the trees out of sight. He turned to tear after them.

Then the scream of a great motor came deafeningly through the air. King was coming down with his blood-red plane, out of twilight skies. He held something in his hand out of the window. It was shaped like a drop of water but was much larger and had fins on the top. It was a bomb.

He screamed over the head of the giant and the giant stopped for a split second to stare. Then the bomb dropped from the window of the cabin and fell straight and true in a slowly decreasing arc.

Bam! The bomb struck the back of the giant's skull. It exploded with a deafening detonation. The concussion hurled those below to the ground. The giant reeled. Then he pitched headlong, smashing the remains of the church to bits as he fell.

King circled and came down to land. He climbed out of the plane and went running over to the scene.

Now for the first time Pennington was coming out of his house.

Luga, with Flo still clutched under his arm, came creeping back stealthily, making sure that the way was clear.

Pennington stared about his beautiful lawn. He shook his head sadly.

"I never would have believed," he said, "that such a thing could happen in this peaceful place. How will it ever be cleared up, th—the—that giant there in the debris of the church. He's thoroughly dead, is he?"

The Key laughed.

"Boy, you'd be dead, too, if you'd had the back of your head blown off."

"Yes," said King, "he's dead all right. I got one of those new high explosive aerial bombs that I heard the army had been experimenting with. I imagine the army can be prevailed upon to clean up the giant just so they can study the effect of the bomb exploding, and as far as the church is concerned, Mr. Pennington, I remember you mentioned not long ago that you were ready to pay anything to have this blackmail menace cleared up."

"Indeed, I did," Pennington said seriously. "Anything you say, young man."

"I'm not thinking of myself," said King, "but there seems to be one congregation near here that's pretty badly in need of a new church. I'm sure we'll be perfectly satisfied if you'll see to it that they get one."

"I will see to it," said Pennington.

A long time later the Secret 6 sat about the great fire in their jungle cabin.

"Well, don't you think it's about time to turn in?" asked the Bishop.

King stared into the fire and smiled.

236

"I think I'll pass it up until I'm sleepier," he said. "I'm sure if I were to go to bed now, I'd do nothing but dream about giants."

The Key laughed. "Holy Gee," he said, "I never realized before what a piker this guy Jack, the giant Killer, was by the side of you, King."

THE SPIDER

- ❏ #1: The Spider Strikes — $13.95
- ❏ #2: The Wheel of Death — $13.95
- ❏ #3: Wings of the Black Death — $13.95
- ❏ #4: City of Flaming Shadows — $13.95
- ❏ #5: Empire of Doom! — $13.95
- ❏ #6: Citadel of Hell — $13.95
- ❏ #7: The Serpent of Destruction — $13.95
- ❏ #8: The Mad Horde — $13.95
- ❏ #9: Satan's Death Blast — $13.95
- ❏ #10: The Corpse Cargo — $13.95
- ❏ #11: Prince of the Red Looters — $13.95
- ❏ #12: Reign of the Silver Terror — $13.95
- ❏ #13: Builders of the Dark Empire — $13.95
- ❏ #14: Death's Crimson Juggernaut — $13.95
- ❏ #15: The Red Death Rain — $13.95
- ❏ #16: The City Destroyer — $13.95
- ❏ #17: The Pain Emperor — $13.95
- ❏ #18: The Flame Master — $13.95
- ❏ #19: Slaves of the Crime Master — $13.95
- ❏ #20: Reign of the Death Fiddler — $13.95
- ❏ #21: Hordes of the Red Butcher — $13.95
- ❏ #22: Dragon Lord of the Underworld — $13.95
- ❏ #23: Master of the Death-Madness — $13.95
- ❏ #24: King of the Red Killers — $13.95
- ❏ #25: Overlord of the Damned — $13.95
- ❏ #26: Death Reign of the Vampire King — $13.95
- ❏ #27: Emperor of the Yellow Death — $13.95
- ❏ #28: The Mayor of Hell — $13.95
- ❏ #29: Slaves of the Murder Syndicate — $13.95
- ❏ #30: Green Globes of Death — $13.95
- ❏ *NEW:* #31: The Cholera King — $13.95

THE MYSTERIOUS WU FANG

- ❏ #1: The Case of the Six Coffins — $12.95
- ❏ #2: The Case of the Scarlet Feather — $12.95
- ❏ #3: The Case of the Yellow Mask — $12.95
- ❏ #4: The Case of the Suicide Tomb — $12.95
- ❏ #5: The Case of the Green Death — $12.95
- ❏ #6: The Case of the Black Lotus — $12.95
- ❏ #7: The Case of the Hidden Scourge — $12.95

G-8 AND HIS BATTLE ACES

- ❏ #1: The Bat Staffel — $13.95

CAPTAIN SATAN

- ❏ #1: The Mask of the Damned — $13.95
- ❏ #2: Parole for the Dead — $13.95
- ❏ #3: The Dead Man Express — $13.95
- ❏ #4: A Ghost Rides the Dawn — $13.95
- ❏ #5: The Ambassador From Hell — $13.95

THE SECRET 6

- ❏ 1: The Red Shadow — $13.95
- ❏ #2: House of Walking Corpses — $13.95
- ❏ *NEW:* #3: The Monster Murders — $13.95

CAPTAIN ZERO

- ❏ #1: City of Deadly Sleep — $13.95
- ❏ #2: The Mark of Zero! — $13.95
- ❏ #3: The Golden Murder Syndicate — $13.95

OPERATOR 5

- ❏ #1: The Masked Invasion — $13.95
- ❏ #2: The Invisible Empire — $13.95
- ❏ #3: The Yellow Scourge — $13.95
- ❏ #4: The Melting Death — $13.95
- ❏ #5: Cavern of the Damned — $13.95
- ❏ #6: Master of Broken Men — $13.95
- ❏ #7: Invasion of the Dark Legions — $13.95
- ❏ #8: The Green Death Mists — $13.95
- ❏ #9: Legions of Starvation — $13.95
- ❏ #10: The Red Invader — $13.95
- ❏ #11: The League of War-Monsters — $13.95
- ❏ #12: The Army of the Dead — $13.95
- ❏ #13: March of the Flame Marauders — $13.95
- ❏ #14: Blood Reign of the Dictator — $13.95
- ❏ #15: Invasion of the Yellow Warlords — $13.95
- ❏ #16: Legions of the Death Master — $13.95

DUSTY AYRES AND HIS BATTLE BIRDS

- ❏ #1: Black Lightning! — $13.95
- ❏ #2: Crimson Doom — $13.95
- ❏ #3: The Purple Tornado — $13.95
- ❏ #4: The Screaming Eye — $13.95
- ❏ #5: The Green Thunderbolt — $13.95
- ❏ #6: The Red Destroyer — $13.95
- ❏ #7: The White Death — $13.95
- ❏ #8: The Black Avenger — $13.95
- ❏ #9: The Silver Typhoon — $13.95
- ❏ #10: The Troposphere F-S — $13.95
- ❏ #11: The Blue Cyclone — $13.95
- ❏ #12: The Tesla Raiders — $13.95

DR. YEN SIN

- ❏ #1: Mystery of the Dragon's Shadow — $12.95
- ❏ #2: Mystery of the Golden Skull — $12.95
- ❏ #3: Mystery of the Singing Mummies — $12.95

MAVERICKS

- ❏ #1: Five Against the Law — $12.95
- ❏ #2: Mesquite Manhunters — $12.95
- ❏ #3: Bait for the Lobo Pack — $12.95
- ❏ #4: Doc Grimson's Outlaw Posse — $12.95
- ❏ #5: Charlie Parr's Gunsmoke Cure — $12.95